THE
SAGA
OF
ILKAY

AND COLLECTED STORIES

THE DRAGOS PRIMERI SERIES

NATALIE WRIGHT

ART & ILLUSTRATIONS BY:

FELIX FARLEY,
CAITLIN INGRALDI &
ANGELINA ROBERTS

MENARIS
BOOKS

TUCSON

Published by Menaris Books, Tucson, Arizona.

LCCN: 2023918739

Hardcover
ISBN: 979-8-9874912-4-9

CONTENTS

Cover Art & Dragon Illustration by Braken

Thundering, a Poem
    By Natalie Wright v

Map, Southern Sulmére Detail
    By Angelina Roberts vii

The Saga of Ilkay
    By Natalie Wright 1

On the Backs of the Ancestors, Illustration
    By Felix Farley 15

The Dragon Confronts Ilkay, Illustration
    By Felix Farley. 35

Dance of Lumine, Illustration
    By Angelina Roberts. 57

To Dance with Lumine, A Poem
    By Natalie Wright. 59

Map, Detail of Bardivia and Vindaô Province
    By Angelina Roberts 67

Portrait of Amantu the Peacock, Illustration
    By Caitlin Ingraldi 71

The Prince and the Peacock
    By Natalie Wright 73

THUNDERING

Thundering hooves,
    a stampede of thirst compels them.

                        We run.

Thundering hearts,
    the forest echo moves me.

                        I wonder.

Thundering sky,
    the biting rain soaks us.

                        They drink.

Shh. Listen.

The deluge drums,
    as roots warble an ancient song.

                        Gods awake.

Come. Gather.

We dance
    in the mud
        we make.

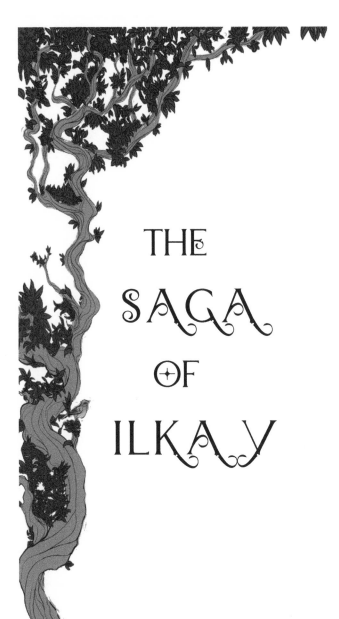

THE
SAGA
OF
ILKAY

CHAPTER I

Ilkay poked the dwindling fire, sending orange embers dancing to the æther. Niyadi's dance with Vay'Nada grew longer each night, and Ilkay shivered at the encroaching shadow time. Her dreaded destination, Volenex, glowed on the horizon like a fiery maw. "Courage, Ilkay," she told herself. "Father's depending on you."

To preserve warmth, Ilkay pulled her arms closer. She wrapped her keffla to ward off the stench from the Phisma tar pits. *I must cross the pits tomorrow.* The prospect made her stomach lurch. Thinking about what she would face sapped her resolve.

The Lord of Chaos tests me. Shadow be stilled. I will not allow you to stop me.

"Besides, what choice do the gods give me?" Ilkay asked the inky night and half expected an answer. Night, the silent specter, had become her only companion on this journey. "Stay strong, papa. Do as our Bruxia says until I return."

She wiped a cold tear, snuffled, and spread her reed pallet for sleep. Ilkay had only a few hours to rest before Big Brother's first light. *I will rise with Hiyadi and continue south. The sooner I face Volenex, the better. For Father and for me.*

Ilkay ventured south not for pleasure, but on a vital mission. Beset by a powerful curse, her father had fallen gravely ill. Neither the bruxia's herbs nor O'Dishi chants had cured him. Hishnari, Bruxia of the village where Ilkay's herdclan summered, said Ilkay would find the remedy at Volenex. Traveling merchants claimed that within the craggy caldera of Volenex was a dragon's lair. Her father had said such talk was silly gossip, but Ilkay shuddered at the idea that the merchant chatter was true. *What am I stepping into?*

It had taken two days to clear the dunes of the mid-Sulmére desert. Behind her, sand blew across the dunes, sounding like a mournful ghost. Ilkay felt a thousand eyes on her. *The ancestors are restless tonight.* Hishnari spoke of nights such as this. When Juka's winds threaten to sunder the veil between the worlds of the living and the dead. Nights when spirit leaks into the world of man.

Ilkay clutched the amber pendant hanging from her neck and whispered a prayer to Lumine, now a slim crescent in the sky. *Watch over me as I sleep, Night's Sister. And send these restless souls to the river to find peace.* She kissed the pendant, a gift from her father, and laid her troubled head to sleep. *Pray Hiyadi's light brings calm.*

The soft whistle of shifting dunes became a roaring gale. When Ilkay woke, sand buried her legs. The sky was blood-red, the winds thrashing and threatening to rip the keffla from her head. *I must ignore the ill-omen in these skies.*

She tore the reed pallet from the accumulated mound of sand and thrust her pack onto her back. Ilkay had no time to think or even break her fast. Without the suns or stars to navigate, she tried to move away from the darkest red sky and toward the less threatening heavens. *Away from the dunes.*

Ilkay pushed her legs forward faster than ever, but Juka's breath pressed against her. *It's as if the wily god of æther does not want me to reach my destination.* Father put little stock in believing that gods are interested in human affairs. Most people, though, believed gods and spirits granted both boons and bad luck, both blessing and bedeviling Menauld. *I don't know if the gods are watching, but just in case they care, I promise, Lumine, to walk the path of Righteous Waters if you guide me safely to Volenex.*

Repeated prayers and reciting the Still Waters mantra did nothing to calm the gale.

Ilkay advanced against the dust storm. Her legs felt as heavy as barrels of ale. Between the sands blotting out Hiyadi's pale morning light and her fully wrapped keffla, Ilkay couldn't see where she was going. She knew only that she must keep moving. If she stopped, she'd perish. *Papa is counting on me.* The thought gave her strength to soldier onward.

Fatigue sapped her resolve, and she wished to lie in the sand and rest. Ilkay played tricks with her own mind to convince herself to continue. When mind tricks no longer worked, she promised herself a sip of water or a bite of food. After what seemed like days, she'd moved beyond the storm's worst. Ilkay unwrapped her keffla just enough to investigate her surroundings.

What is that? Ilkay paused, spying a dark, rounded hump on the horizon. *Is it a hut? But that is impossible.* Even with Juka's winds raging, Ilkay caught the odor of the Phisma pits. *No one would build a house here.*

The possibility of shelter gave Ilkay hope and reinvigorated her more than mind tricks, water, or even food. Her legs still wobbly, Ilkay picked up speed as she rushed toward the dark mound.

As she got closer, Ilkay realized the knoll was not a hut, soil, or rock. It was the empty shell of what had been a large ranju. *It's so large a small family could live inside. I will shelter here and rest until the storm has fully passed.*

The neck opening was a dark hole. She couldn't see beyond the neck hole in the still-dim light. *I hope no beast has already claimed this shell as its home.* She ignored the thought and stepped inside, pressing herself against the shell.

With the carapace hugging her back, Ilkay slid to the ground, her knees to her chest. Though dark and dank, like the meat cellar back home, the empty ranju shell comforted her. Relief brought a tear to Ilkay's eye. She pulled the water sac from her side, her hands shaky as she allowed herself a long draw of precious water. Ilkay drank at least two portions in a long gulp. *I will worry about rations after my body stops trembling.*

Ready to bite into her dried thukna meat, something brushed against her. Ilkay sprang to her feet in one swift move and began backing out of the shell. She fumbled with the scabbard at her waist but finally retrieved her palkurba blade. Ilkay's heart pounded like a stampeding thukna herd, and the palkurba shook in her hand.

Several possibilities for what had moved at her side flitted in her mind. Wild dogs, giant sand snakes, man-sized poisonous lizards, and even desert wolves roamed these lands. But wild beasts were the least of her concerns. Pesha frightened her more. *What if this shell is home to a dishonored, clanless person?*

"Show yourself." Despite the generous drink of water, Ilkay's voice sounded like dried herbs being crushed.

Something inside the shell rustled, and Ilkay took a few steps backward. As she considered whether she should run, the bottom of the shell rose from the dirt.

And from the dark opening into which she had sought shelter, a huge, age-weathered head emerged. An elderly ranju blinked his milky eyes so slowly that the old desert tortoise appeared to move in slow motion. His beak nose, nearly as large as a small child, was now only an arm's length from Ilkay.

The ranju continued to blink, clearing the sleep from his ancient eyes. *How long has he been sleeping?* Ranju lived longer than anything else in the Sulmére. The old ranju might have lived in her great-grandfather's time or longer.

"I meant you no harm. I only sought to shelter from Juka's rage."

His eyes were now fully open, and though covered in a pale film, he focused keenly on Ilkay. "Who are you? And if you mean no harm, why do you brandish a blade at old Oshon'Zahar, hmm?" Oshon'Zahar's voice was deep, resonating in her chest, and raspy from disuse.

Even though she held the palkurba with both hands, the blade quivered. "I am Ilkay, and I was afraid. I did not know what manner of beast had taken shelter in your shell." Ranjus were known for peacefully going about their business, paying no heed to human endeavors. She couldn't recall a single tale or legend of a hero fighting off a ranju, so she lowered her blade.

Oshon'Zahar blinked and pulled his beak away from her. "What do you run from that you are near the pits, cowering inside my home?"

Ilkay disliked the insinuation that she was cowardly. "I'm not running from anything." She pulled herself up as she stowed the palkurba in its scabbard. "I journey to Volenex."

The shifting sand beneath them shook as Oshon'Zahar laughed, his mirth like the low rumble of distant but mighty thunder. "Are you a fool or intent on ending yourself before this harsh life does?" He laughed again.

First, he infers cowardice, and now he laughs at me. "Look here. I am neither a coward nor a fool. My quest is noble, and my time runs thin. I apologize for disturbing your slumber, but I must cross the pits today. I have no time to trade insults."

"Every fool thinks his ends are just."

Ilkay harrumphed and stood tall and defiant. "I will make amends to Lumine for naysaying my revered elder—but you, Oshon'Zahar, are a fool if you think it folly to save a life."

The old tortoise turned his clearer right eye toward her and moved closer as if trying to take measure of her. "Someone so important you'd risk your life in the bowels of Menauld at Volenex? Were you commanded to save a ruler or perhaps a master?"

In the time spent speaking to this crusty tortoise, my father's life wanes. The thought brought hot tears. "Though he rules nothing but his own conscience, he is like Hiyadi's warm light on my face in the morn and Lumine's loving arms as I sleep at night."

Oshon'Zahar nodded his magnificent head once. "I am corrected by youth and shamed for assuming so little of you."

Admission of shame by such a wise old creature was unexpected. "Now we know something of each other. And no apology is necessary. I entered your home without permission. But time is of the essence. I must go." Ilkay bowed her head and headed south again.

"If you don't know where to step, you will perish."

Ilkay sucked in a breath to calm herself. *We just made peace with one another. I don't want to erupt, but he rankles me.* Ilkay managed a calm voice. "Thank you for reminding me of the likelihood of my imminent demise, but I must try. Wouldn't you?"

Oshon'Zahar lowered his head, his beak nearly touching the soil. He closed his eyes, and it looked as though he'd gone to sleep. At last, he gazed up. Oshon'Zahar said, "You do not know where to step. But I do." He sighed. "I have lived long in solitude. Left with no purpose but to merely exist." Oshon'Zahar extended his long neck, his right eye now mere inches from hers. "Oshon'Zahar will help you survive the Phisma pits."

He turned south with an agility unnatural for such an enormous creature. Oshon'Zahar craned his thin neck and asked her, "Are your legs stuck in the sand?"

Once again, hope empowered her to deny the thirst, hunger, and weariness that threatened to undo her. Ilkay hurried after the hulking Oshon'Zahar, gladdened to have a companion to guide her through the perilous pits.

CHAPTER 2

Ilkay's legs had been like mushy tubers, but Oshon'Zahar's promise of help made her forget the fatigue. Oshon'Zahar moved more gracefully and quickly than Ilkay. Her breaths were labored, and she struggled to keep up with the old ranju.

Fortunately, they came to the edge of the Phisma pits before Hiyadi was midway to zenith. The scrub and sand gave way to bubbling black ooze. The pits stretched to the horizon. Tiny islands dotted the sea of black tar, bits of land that had not yet sunk into the mire. Most of the "islands" were barely large enough for a foothold and spaced further apart than a human step.

The Phisma pit's foul odor assaulted Ilkay's nose, and she wrapped her keffla again and pinched her nostrils. *By Lumine's light, this must be Vay'Nada's work.* "By the Three. The stench will end me before I cross this evil pit." *Hishnari, you may be Bruxia, but even you could not have known how rank these pits are, or you would not have sent me.*

Oshon'Zahar's low voice rumbled as he laughed. "Fear not, child. Oshon'Zahar knows the way."

Ilkay surveyed the bubbling ooze stretching as far as she could see. She could not identify a pattern or path. "What's the trick for traversing this foul pit of Vay'Nada's breath?"

"There are no shortcuts through the darkness. Your only tools? Knowledge and trust in the ancestors."

The great tortoise lowered his eyelids and pulled his thin neck back into his shell until only the tip of his beak showed. Oshon'Zahar sang, mumbled words warbling from his throat in an ancient tongue that Ilkay could not understand.

Deep, resonant tones rumbled in Ilkay's belly. Though she didn't understand the words, Oshon'Zahar's song calmed her. Her eyelids grew heavy. She blinked slowly, trying to stay awake as Oshon'Zahar sang an ancient tune. Through slitted eyes, Ilkay imagined land rising from the tarry sea that stretched before them.

The ground shook, and Ilkay nearly toppled over. She was wide awake now and rubbed her eyes. The rising mounds of land had been no dream. By the time Oshon'Zahar finished his song, once sparse dots of land had become ample hillocks. A path lay before her.

"By the Three, what magic is this?" she whispered. She kissed two fingers and made the crescent sign on her forehead to ward off evil.

"The oldest of magic," Oshon'Zahar said. The great tortoise lowered his neck, swooping it down until it nearly touched the soil. "Climb on my back, Ilkay. Trust that I will not falter as we walk this path together."

Though there were plentiful footholds now across the black sea, Ilkay was happy for Oshon'Zahar's aid. *He is large but steady on his feet.* Her legs wobbled like a drey-milk custard as she scrambled atop his back.

Oshon'Zahar set out methodically, stepping carefully from one dark, rounded mound to the next. Though the newly risen land provided abundant space for footfalls, they were slick with gooey tar. But the ancient tortoise did not waver. He slowly but steadily moved with certitude into the Phisma tar pits.

After a time, Ilkay asked, "How did you command the land to rise and create these islands?"

Oshon'Zahar chuckled, the sound vibrating his shell beneath Ilkay's bottom. "I command nothing." He laughed again. "That's why human magic remains rudimentary. They think it is about command and control." He tsked.

Ilkay never thought about magic. She lived a humble life in the Sulmére sands. A place where your next meal comes from hard-working hands. Where people value practical knowledge, like where to find water during a drought. Bruxia healing arts are well-respected. But human magic, like they study at the Pillars, is used primarily for wars waged by wealthy people from the capitals. Of no value in the Sulmére.

Finally, she said, "You did not answer my question, Oshon'Zahar. How did you make the land rise?"

"We do not walk on land but tread on the backs of my ancestors."

"Are you saying these knolls are..." Ilkay glanced around at the curved mounds around them. As she paid closer attention, the truth of what Oshon'Zahar said became obvious. The tar-covered hillocks were roughly the same size and shape as Oshon'Zahar's back. "But how?"

"Before Vay'Nada corrupted Volenex, it was once a fertile land by the sea. My ancestors, lured by spring's warm seas and tender shoots, crossed the Phisma pits to get to this verdant land."

Ilkay tried to count the shells, but the number was too great to reckon. "If so many perished, why keep going?"

"You live in the Sulmére. You know what a harsh mother she can be. If your kin knew of a promised land—where you could eat until your bellies were full. Where your young would never know hunger. Would you not chase this dream? Even if it meant risk to your life?"

Ilkay silently considered his words. Though her herdclan thrived by following spring's snowmelt to the sea and back again each year, many a young babe died from hunger, thirst, or lack of Bruxia healing while ranging. She stared at the horizon, bleak and wavering with the day's heat. There were no verdant hills of green, but she imagined her herdclan would gladly risk death to gain fertile lands so they would never know hunger.

"All these ranju died on the journey?"

"Many ranju perished, that is certain. But most of the revered backs on which we walk belonged to elderly and infirm who volunteered to create a path for their kin."

Ilkay gasped. "Volunteered?" A shiver up her spine made her pull her arms tighter to her sides for warmth. "They willingly allowed this Vay'Nada pit to swallow them—alive?"

Oshon'Zahar nodded slowly. "It was a different time, Ilkay. My ancestors lived in large communities, not lone wanderers as I am today."

His voice was a lament. Ranju shells stretched as far as the horizon. The shimmering tar wavered through Ilkay's tears.

"And they serve even to this day," she whispered.

Oshon'Zahar nodded again. "It is not for me to command souls who made the ultimate sacrifice. Instead, the magic is simple and as old as magic itself. I simply love them and honor them. This is the only payment required to open the path through darkness."

Ilkay wiped her dusty face with her sleeve. "It's so simple, yet so powerful. Such magic could help so many. Why don't people know about this?"

"Your kin have always had access to this ancient magic. But your people value only what makes them wealthy or powerful."

Instead of taking offense to Oshon'Zahar's slight of her people, Ilkay said a silent prayer. She did not pray to her own ancestors, for what Oshon'Zahar said was true. Instead, she offered prayers to the ranju ancestors upon whose backs they trod.

Swaying gently on Oshon'Zahar's back, Ilkay nodded off. When she woke, the horizon had changed. They were almost to the edge of the Phisma pits, and ahead loomed a craggy black mountain range, the sky above it the color of fire. To the east, steam billowed from the sea as Vay'Nada's angry magma spilled into the water. Smoke poured from the crater of the angry mountain Volenex, said to be the home of an ancient beast who held the key to her father's life. Her throat tightened, and her stomach roiled.

As if sensing her fear, Oshon'Zahar said, "Remember, Vay'Nada uses tricks of our mind to put fear in our hearts. What do you see before you?"

Before Ilkay could answer, Oshon'Zahar continued. "Smoke. Steam and vapors. A strong wind could blow it away and reveal there's nothing behind it but water and rock."

I know he tries to calm me, but I fear what lies beneath the water and what lives within the rock. But Ilkay recalled words of encouragement she once heard from her father. *"Fear not the beast's fires, Ilkay, for Lumine blessed you with the Waters of Life. Carry them in your heart always, for the Shadow feeds on chaos and fears nothing more than the glassy stillness of calm waters."*

Ilkay whispered the Still Waters mantra. "Mind calm. Still Waters. Heart sure. Still Waters. Breathe easy. Still Waters." She repeated it quietly to herself several times.

Usually, repetition of the mantra and some deep breaths calmed any disturbance of her mind. But staring at the angry mountain ahead, Still Waters had little effect on her racing thoughts and hard-beating heart.

Oshon'Zahar stepped from the last ancient ranju shell. He lifted his cloudy eyes upward to gaze upon the towering, black, craggy peak of Volenex and sniffed the air. "Something foul taints the air here."

"You mean something other than tar, lava, and the stench of dead fish?" Ilkay slid from Oshon'Zahar's back and stretched, then double-wrapped her keffla. Thankfully, the powerful odor of huson pine lingered in the fabric's weave and masked some of the scent.

"I know that smell, though it has been long since I've encountered it." He gazed at Ilkay, and his previously calm demeanor gave way to wide-eyed fear. "Though your purpose is noble, I urge you to reconsider."

Ilkay gave a wry laugh. "Now? After hours of traversing the nasty tar. Days since I knew the comforts of my home and hearth and kin. Now you say to turn back. Why?"

Oshon'Zahar craned his neck toward her until his beak nearly touched her nose. "The beast you seek slumbers in the deep belly of Volenex. But I smell Nixan shifters of the foulest sort. Raven-black hair, nails like claws, and tongues as slippery as eels in oil."

All children were told stories of slints, a type of Nixan changeling said to steal children in the night. But Ilkay assumed the stories were just that—legends told to frighten little ones into staying near their parents and kin. "Nixan truly exist?"

Oshon'Zahar gave a single, slow nod. "These Vay'Nada spawn are tricky ones, using their silver tongue language to pry from their victims what they would not give willingly. And if that does not work, they rip the poor sot to shreds and devour their heart."

Ilkay gulped and broke into a cold sweat. *Hishnari did not tell me of Nixan. Maybe she did not know about them.* Or perhaps she feared revealing what Oshon'Zahar had because then Ilkay might not embark on the journey. "Have you encountered them before?"

He shook his head. "I last sensed this odor when I was no older than you." His voice was wistful. "Several human lifetimes ago. A long time, even for a ranju." He blinked and brought his gaze back to Ilkay. "The mountain was not angry then, and sweet green shoots covered the slopes in spring. We crossed the pits that year for the last time as one unified ranju clan. As we neared, elders called us back from the mountain. We lost over two dozen of our kin that day. I will never forget the frightened cries of the babies. The moans of agony from my fallen elders. And worse still, the horrid stench of Nixan attackers."

Ilkay considered Oshon'Zahar's words, and she shook with fear. "Your advice is sound, and your fears, I'm sure, are justified. But Oshon'Zahar, what choice do I have? My father will die if I do not retrieve the cure for the curse. Even worse, he will carry this vile hex into his next life. The curse will forever taint his soul." She sniffled and wiped her eyes. "If that happens, we will never meet again by Lumine's waters. My quest might be hopeless, Oshon'Zahar, but I must try. What would you do?"

The old ranju closed his eyes and breathed deeply, then nuzzled Ilkay's arm with his beak. "Go. Oshon'Zahar will wait. Triumphant with the cure in your hand, I will ferry you across." His voice was brighter now, as if the dire need of Ilkay's situation gave him resolve.

When Ilkay did not move to leave, he nudged her again. "Go, my friend. It is an opportune time. I promise to wait for you."

"But it could be days. I pray it does not take weeks, but it could."

Oshon'Zahar chuckled, his deep, rumbling laugh a balm for Ilkay's worried heart. "What are human weeks to an old ranju like me?" He gently nudged her again. "Go, Ilkay, before you lose the will."

Ilkay wiped her eyes with the back of her hand, adjusted her pack, took a deep breath, and wrapped her arms around Oshon'Zahar's wrinkly neck. "Thank you, Oshon'Zahar. I treasure you." She kissed the tip of his beak. "May the Brothers grace you with their warmth all of your days."

She turned toward her destination, her legs wobbly and her mind fevered with fear. Behind her, Oshon'Zahar called, "And may the Sister welcome you in her arms."

The words eased some of her fear, and she was grateful for the ranju's reply. She walked backward and asked him, "Have you any advice for when I face the Nixan?"

His reply was swift and sure. "To survive your encounter with Nixan, give them what they want."

Ilkay waved goodbye and took his words to heart. "I have little to offer. But I will give what I must to preserve my father's soul."

She marched toward the angry mountain and left the Phisma pits and Oshon'Zahar's kind heart behind. "I am as ready as I can be to face Volenex's dangers."

CHAPTER 3

The stench of the Phisma tar pits waned as Ilkay neared the towering black crags of Volenex. Even in the Brothers' mid-day light, Volenex loomed like a dark specter. Her relief at surviving the pits disappeared. Even in the dunes, plants plunge deep roots to tap hidden moisture and survive. In the bleak shadow of Volenex, though, nothing lived. *Vay'Nada scours Menauld of all life. I hope it does not sweep me away as well.*

As Ilkay neared the volatile mountain, she longed for the relatively blissful odor of tar. Here, the sea boiled, and tides brought rotting fish to the outer edges of the mighty mountain. Smoke from the caldera blotted out the twin suns and cast an eerie yellow-orange haze. The roiling caldera added sulfur to the odor of rotting fish. *If only I could close my nose to the stench like I close my eyes to things I wish not to see.*

Even Juka dared not tread in the shadow of Volenex. The air was unnaturally stagnant and forbidding. Heat rising from the wrathful ground made the air shimmer, and rivers of sweat poured down Ilkay's back.

She stopped for a ration of water and thukna jerky, mindful to not take too greedy a portion. The water was wet but hot and not as refreshing as she wished. As she chewed, a rock-eagle's call pierced the quiet.

What in the name of the Three is a rock-eagle doing out here? She searched the skies but did not see the bird circling. Soon, another call, this time a raven. The distinct 'brock-brock' added to the whistling cry of the rock-eagle.

Ilkay stowed her rations and trudged on, fueled by curiosity. As she hiked, more bird calls joined the first two. Before long, the cacophony of bird squawks, cries, and songs made her wish for something to plug her ears.

She'd been unable to see the birds creating the noise. Now, entirely in the shadow of the towering black walls of Volenex, Ilkay spied at least two dozen birds of prey circling. The birds were unnaturally large. Some were the size of small people or even larger.

Ilkay grabbed the amber pendant through her clothing and whispered a prayer. "Lumine, preserve me." *They must be Nixan changelings like Oshon'Zahar warned of. What else could explain their unnatural size?*

The birds circled not over Volenex itself but at its northern edge. Ilkay moved cautiously, trying not to catch the attention of the flying beasts. She kept her eyes trained ahead, looking for a path to climb up the mountain and access the inner caldera.

Attempts to escape notice failed. The ungainly flock descended. As the rock eagle landed, it morphed into a woman. Soon, the other birds touched down, and each became a person until there were nearly thirty women of varying ages, from girls just entering womanhood to aged crones perhaps older than Hishnari.

With beady black eyes and glistening black hair, even in human form, these Nixan appeared bird-like. They wore ratty, tattered clothes, and their fingernails were ragged claws. The Nixan encircled Ilkay, sniffing and staring like she would be their next meal.

Ilkay clutched harder at her pendant, even as her innards threatened to let loose. She whispered another prayer to the Sister and repeated Still Waters softly to herself. "What do you want of me?" she asked.

Soaring above, the rock eagle had been graceful and magnificent. As a woman, though, she was bent with age, her face spotted and her hair sparse like threads of grey silk clinging to her head. When she spoke, her voice was like dried reeds in the wind. "Are you a young sorcerer from the Pillars?"

What an odd question. I do not wear the Trinity mark upon my forehead nor don the colors of a Pillar. "I do not know the ways of Menaris."

The throng of women sniffed and tsked. Some even cackled. *Did I say something amusing?*

The rock-eagle spoke again. "What business have you at Volenex?"

Ilkay's first instinct was to lie, though it was not her natural way. Something about the scent and cloying stares of the women made her want to hold secret everything she held dear. Oshon'Zahar's words came to mind. *"These Vay'Nada spawn are tricky ones, using their silver tongue language to pry from their victims what they would not give willingly. If that does not work, they rip the poor sot to shreds and devour their heart."*

Against both instinct and the wise old ranju's dire warning, Ilkay spoke the truth. "I have journeyed far and survived much hardship, not on a lark or fool's folly, but to seek that which will break the terrible curse upon the one I love most. If you are the guardians of Volenex, I pray you let me pass, for the cure I seek lies within."

To this statement, the collected Nixan chittered and murmured as they drew closer to Ilkay. The rock-eagle smiled, showing yellowed teeth covered in a brackish-green oily film. "A hero then, on a noble quest." She cackled, and a cacophony of sickly laughing made Ilkay cover her ears.

Are they laughing at me? Perhaps they know what Oshon'Zahar warned. Maybe I am on a fool's errand, after all. But what choice do I have? Ilkay had journeyed far already and still not found the cure she sought.

"Laugh, if you will, but within these stone walls lies a beast. And from this beast, I must take something that it willingly gives. I will not leave until I have what I came for."

"We give you no reason to be indignant, youngling. Your cause is just, and it aligns with our own."

That Ilkay's purpose aligned with the cause of these Vay'Nada spawn gave no comfort. Despite the sultry heat, Ilkay shivered. She swallowed hard and asked a question she feared knowing the answer to. "And what is your purpose at Volenex?"

The Nixan shrieked and laughed, chittered, and some sang an odd, plaintive tune. They moved even closer, so near now that Ilkay smelled their fetid odor, like dank earth mixed with garbage and peat.

"The beast you seek is a dragon. He slumbers within the walls of the inner caldera. You will never make it into his lair though. One must fly to reach it."

From the gathered Nixan rose a chorus of, "But we fly, we fly, we fly."

Ilkay's stomach churned at the idea of allowing herself to be carried in the claws of a Nixan. *Like a baby drey being led to slaughter.* An image of her ill father sprang to mind. "Are you offering to take me there? What price do you demand in return?"

The rock-eagle leaned close. Her rank breath made Ilkay pull back. "A price will be paid. Oh yes. We will have what is ours." Her beady eyes grew even darker. She smacked her shriveled lips. "You are merely a conduit, youngling. Have no fear."

Conduit? The Nixan told her not to fear, yet her tone held no comfort. "Speak plainly. What use will you make of me?"

More cackles and shrieks pierced the air, along with quiet whispers and clacking of their nails. The rock eagle said, "Do not fret. Though we long to shred your flesh and feast your tender heart, you are too valuable to devour."

Ilkay sensed the rock eagle's pronouncement was less to allay Ilkay's fears than to warn her sisters not to feast on Ilkay. A few groaned, and others made unhappy noises.

"Put plainly, the slumbering dragon protected his lair with enchantments to ward off Vay'Nada's creatures. Humankind is no threat. You lack the skill to survive Volenex's imposing fortress and the knowledge of the ancient magics to break the spell. Thus, the mighty one did not set wards against human encroachment."

The bargain was becoming apparent. "So, you can't set foot—or wing—within the walls of Volenex. But I can? You need a human to speak the spell to break the wards?"

The Nixan cried out. Some morphed back into bird form and circled overhead. The rock-eagle said, "You can speak the words to sever the wards. Once we breach the defenses, we will carry you to the inner sanctum of the beast."

Turning the plot around in her mind, Ilkay could not see a hidden path to her destruction. *Unless they intend to shred my skin once they have what they want.* "How do I know you will not simply dispose of me once I've spoken the words to defeat the wards?"

The rock-eagle regarded her coolly and appeared to ponder what assurance she could provide. She then plucked a mottled creamy white and brown feather from her tatty hair and handed it to Ilkay. "A piece of myself, freely given. It marks you under my protection. Should you defeat the barrier, I will protect you from the beast slumbering within this mountain. And from my sisters' ravenous appetite."

Ilkay reluctantly took the feather from the old woman's hand. She was in the belly of Vay'Nada, subject to the Shadow's chaotic whims. *I need all the protection I can get. But I fear a hidden price I will one day regret.* "We have a bargain. I will speak these words and sever the fiery beast's defenses. In exchange, you will take me to parlay with the monster."

The rock-eagle revealed her craggy teeth again in a broad smile, then let out an ear-splitting cry. The others joined, and most took bird form and circled high above.

Though their enormous forms overhead unsettled Ilkay, she was relieved they no longer pressed near. One Nixan flew too close to the edge of the magical barrier and screeched as an invisible force singed its wings. On the ground, Nixan onlookers cackled at their sister's misfortune. None rushed to give her aid. *A harsh lot, these Nixan.*

In small portions, the rock-eagle spoke the ward-breaking spell. Even then, Ilkay struggled to form the sounds. The language was foreign. The rock-eagle demanded she repeat the incantation several times, correcting her pronunciations, though Ilkay did not know what the strange words meant. *This seems unlikely to work. I do not comprehend what I say.*

"What am I speaking?"

The rock eagle gave her a sideways glance. "I cannot translate the exact meaning into the common tongue, for it is magical. All you need to know is that these ancient words release the barrier that bars Vay'Nada's children from entering."

Finally, the rock eagle was content that Ilkay's delivery of the incantation was adequate to remove the ward. Ilkay lifted her voice to the skies. She spoke with as much conviction as she could muster. She mouthed the spell of breaking, her mouth contorting into unnatural shapes to form the tongue clicks and exceedingly long vowel sounds the ancient language required.

The rock-eagle fed Ilkay the words and demanded she repeat the spell three times. Ilkay did as asked, and by the end line, her jaw was sore.

The barrier had been invisible. There was only one way to determine if the incantation worked. A Nixan must fly through. The elderly changelings shooed one of the younger ones and yowled at her until she donned her feathered form—a sleek, spare falcon. She circled at the edge a few times, perhaps gaining courage. At last, she pressed her head down and forward, her beak jutting out. She flew over the edge of the black spires and beyond where the other Nixan had singed her wing.

The falcon woman soared high and screeched her victory for all below. Soon, flapping stirred the air as the other Nixan took wing.

Before morphing back into a bird, the rock-eagle smiled at Ilkay and said, "You have done us a great service, youngling. Hold tight to my gift. I suggest you look ahead, not down." Her visage changed from an elderly crone to a magnificent, strong-beaked bird. She swooped her neck down, inviting Ilkay to ride on her back.

Ilkay's legs were like mush, and her innards a roiling cauldron, but she had come too far to cave to fear. She hoisted onto the rock eagle's back and reluctantly wrapped her arms around the bird's sturdy neck.

The giant bird flapped its wings as it hopped forward and took flight. Ilkay's stomach felt like it had fallen to her toes. She cried out in surprise as the rock eagle soared up and up and finally over the edge of the outer peaks.

Once above the jagged rock, Ilkay knew the Nixan had told the truth. From the sky, the strength of the fortress's defense came into view. *I likely would not have gotten past the initial peaks.*

The outer peaks, like black jagged glass ready to cut anyone who entered, were only the first layer. Beyond lay a moat of simmering sea, heat shimmering above the bubbling water. *If I attempted to swim across, that sea would cook me alive. Besides, I do not know how to swim.*

Then, beyond the wet tempest, an inner caldera rose. Though Volenex no longer spewed magma from its core, smoke still curled into the sky, evidence that the mountain was still very much alive.

The rock eagle flew with haste, and they soon cleared the burning waters and peaks of the inner caldera. Below them, an ash-covered mound stood out from the jagged surrounding rock. *Is it the barrow of the beast?*

The Nixan surrounded the giant mound and made room for the rock eagle to land. Ilkay tumbled from the bird's back and stumbled into the ash-covered dirt. She wiped the soot from her behind but was thankful for the ash beneath her. The relatively soft layer protected her feet from being cut or burned by the searing, jagged stone.

The rock eagle joined the others as they became ragged women once again. They opened their mouths in unison and sang a horrendous, ear-splitting song. Their voices rattled Ilkay's chest. The sound was more than a song or cry. It was magic, unlike any Ilkay had ever heard of.

They linked arms and moved ever closer to the mound without letting up on their shrill song. The sound of it unnerved Ilkay and made her stomach so uneasy that she retched. Yet the Nixan did not ease up. Instead, their rhythm grew more intense, their voices ever louder.

After what seemed like a lifetime of enduring the awful sound, the mound shook. Across the center appeared a crack and then another.

Does the beast awake?

Ilkay was both frightened and curious. A giant chunk of dusty rock flew from the mound, and an ash-covered snout as large as a full-grown thukna bull poked out. A big eyelid blinked slowly, revealing an amber-yellow eye still hazy with sleep. The beast pushed its head from the mound. It yowled, and the sound quaked the ground.

As large as several full-grown men, the dragon shook its massive head making smoky ash and dirt fill the air. Visible now under the centuries-old layers of grime, the dragon's scales shone deep purple-black, its beard, hair, and whiskers dark as a raven's feathers.

It rotated its giant head, taking in the Nixan surrounding him. At last, the dragon's gaze landed on Ilkay.

The dragon's voice was weak from disuse and barely a whisper. He spoke in the common tongue. "Child, what have you done?"

CHAPTER 4

I t had been weeks since Ilkay left the comforts of home to seek the dragon's lair. In that time, she had imagined the encounter would happen dozens of ways, from the beast eating her in one gulp to burning her to a cinder. She had never imagined the dragon would speak to her.

His tone held neither anger nor hatred but was plaintive and reproachful. He spoke to Ilkay like he was scolding a child for misbehaving.

But the relative peace between the two lasted only a few moments. The massive dragon rose from the mound and unfurled his wings. Above the din of the frantic Nixan came a sound like a bubbling cauldron. The dragon reared back its head, eyed Ilkay, and aimed his open mouth at her, revealing rows of giant teeth.

As Ilkay realized the beast intended to burn her alive with its fiery breath, the rock-eagle spoke in the odd, ancient language. *"Zhijnatu, Vahgrin."* Then she and the others changed the frequency of their horrendous song, and the mighty dragon closed his maw and cowered away from them.

Vahgrin flapped his giant wings, and ash dust filled the air. The dragon's wings made wind, swirling even more dirt, dust, and debris into the air. Ilkay coughed. Some of the younger Nixan coughed too. The older Nixan, though, did not cease their unholy song.

Two young Nixan, their eyes wide and gleaming with exultant excitement, stood so close to the dragon that his dusty beard swept their hair. They pitched their voices high and crooned at his face.

Vahgrin was not cowed. With a decisive swipe of his front claws, he snatched both neophyte Nixan and devoured them whole. Only a pile of black feathers and blood spatters remained of the two neophytes.

Ilkay expected the remaining Nixan to move back from him out of fear they would be his next meal. Instead, they pushed closer. They showed no apparent unrest or melancholy over the loss of their sisters. *These creatures are surely Vay'Nada's own. They have no loyalty or love for one another.*

Vahgrin resisted their attempts to be near him and flapped his mighty wings again. Once he built momentum, Vahgrin took to the air. He was not graceful like the Nixan birds but lumbering and unsteady. *Perhaps he is stiff from years of sleep.*

As ungainly as he was, Vahgrin's giant wings were strong. In mere moments, he rose halfway up the inner caldera.

The Nixan, though, were not content to allow him to escape. They morphed and rose into the air, too. Even in bird form, they continued vocalizing their discordant tune.

On the ground, the rock eagle remained in human form, and along with five other crones, they screamed at Vahgrin in their ancient tongue. "Zhijnatu, Vahgrin." They continued repeating the phrase while their sisters sang their aggressive song at him.

Through air foggy with dust, Ilkay witnessed the Nixan women subdue the mighty beast. *Maybe they cause him pain too great to withstand.* The Nixan forced Vahgrin back to the ground.

Once he landed, the Nixan circled him again and continued their horrid, unrelenting song. At once fearsome, the giant dragon bowed his head and genuflected to the strange bird women. He wore a grimace, his eyes closed, his brow pinched.

He is in pain. Ilkay had prepared herself to battle this beast—even to take its life if she must—to survive and return home with her father's cure. She had not expected to feel pity for the creature.

"What are you doing to him?" Ilkay asked.

The rock-eagle did not answer Ilkay but continued her magical song. But a young Nixan, perhaps no older than Ilkay, said, "We perform the rend. The dragon cannot resist us now. He will obey our command."

"What will you command him to do?"

The young Nixan smiled. "We have grand plans." Her lips formed a giant oval, and she emitted a piercing note.

Vahgrin knelt, his giant neck and head on the ground. The Nixan gathered around him, closer and closer in a tight circle. Several younger Nixan clambered onto Vahgrin's back, letting out throaty yells of victory. Vahgrin devoured no more of the women.

The Nixan crones placed their hands on Vahgrin's grime-covered scales, reverently stroking him while continuing their relentless song of the rend. With an ardent, almost loving gaze, the rock-eagle rubbed Vahgrin's scaly snout as she continued her unbearable song.

Vahgrin glared at the rock-eagle with a look of utter disdain. Like a dog trained to obey its master, the mighty dragon was submissive to the Nixan. His rueful expression, though, revealed the outcome displeased him.

The rock eagle ceased her horrid song. She whispered to Vahgrin. Ilkay could not hear what the woman said. Whatever it was, the words stoked such sadness in the dragon that he shed a tear. A single enormous teardrop dangled from Vahgrin's giant eye.

"Now, Ilkay. Here is the prize you seek. Take it, for he will not give another," the rock-eagle said.

"You must retrieve from the beast that which is freely given," Hishnari had said.

Ilkay rummaged in her pack with shaky hands and retrieved an empty water skin. The unsettling Nixan magical song laid Vahgrin low, but Ilkay's legs still quaked as she approached him.

"Hurry," the rock-eagle hissed. "You get this chance only once. Take it."

Ilkay held the open spout up to Vahgrin's eyelid, and the briny moisture oozed into her water sac and nearly filled it. She secured the lid and held the precious liquid tightly. *I only hope this indeed cures my father.*

In a low voice, still thin and raspy, Vahgrin said, "You hold the prize you sought, but know this. You have awakened me from a self-imposed slumber and unleashed Vay'Nada's shadow upon the land. You know not what you do. Your world will soon suffer from your greed."

The dragon turned from her as though she were unworthy of his attention. His words, an accusation of greed, pierced Ilkay deeply. *How can he accuse me of greed? I risked my life several times over to save my father's life. This is love, not greed.* Yet again, she felt scolded. Like she should have known not to make the bargain with the Nixan.

The Nixan were too busy reveling in their victory to pay her any mind. Ilkay feared that, eventually, hunger would make them turn covetous eyes on her. *I must make haste to return this cure to Hishnari to prepare for my father. I only hope I am not too late.*

The rock eagle was still singing her rend, though not as loudly as before. Ilkay feared retribution for interrupting. But she was no more able to survive Volenex's formidable defenses now than when she arrived. Ilkay gently touched the rock-eagle's wiry arm. "Please. I need your help to leave this place. Will you allow me upon your back once again to get beyond Volenex?"

In a trance-like stare, the rock-eagle slowly turned toward Ilkay. "Even better, youngling. Vahgrin and I both will take you."

Ilkay shuddered. "Vahgrin?" *I dislike where she leads with this idea.*

The rock-eagle screeched at the young Nixan on Vahgrin's back. They tumbled off and scattered, sending disapproving looks for ending their fun.

The old Nixan vaulted onto Vahgrin's back, revealing an impossible agility given her human body's apparent frailty. Once settled just behind Vahgrin's neck, she ordered others to help Ilkay up.

Ilkay had nearly soiled her small clothes when she'd flown on the rock-eagle's back. Her stomach churned like the magma deep beneath them, and she battled the urge to retch.

The rock-eagle issued a command, but the collective Nixan screeching drowned out her words. Vahgrin flapped his mighty wings, and several Nixan fell over from the unexpected powerful gust.

He lifted off, and Ilkay again felt like she left her guts on the ground. She grabbed a handful of Vahgrin's black mane in each hand and held on for dear life.

Vahgrin soared skyward, leaving the hot, malodorous caldera below. His wings flapped quickly, and his body swung downward, then up, repeatedly, as he tried to remain aloft.

To Ilkay, it felt like they would plummet from the sky. But with each flap, the dragon gained strength. Soon, they soared over the roiling moat, and with just a few strokes of his wings at full span, Vahgrin cleared the craggy peaks of Volenex.

The rock-eagle spoke again to Vahgrin, a command Ilkay could not comprehend. Within a few moments, thunder pounded, though there were no storm clouds. Ahead, the sky shimmered like mid-day heat rising from the desert. Ilkay caught the scent of sky-fire, though she'd not seen lightning pierce the sky.

The wavering sky became like a giant eye. At its center, Ilkay saw land. *That is impossible. What Shadow magic is this?* The land at the center of the flickering eye was Ilkay's village. *My home.* Vahgrin headed into the strange vortex and toward where everyone Ilkay loved dwelled.

She clutched her amber pendant. "Three protect us."

Having heard Ilkay's entreaty to her gods, the rock-eagle cackled. "The Three." She laughed. "One day, Ilkay, the old gods will rise. The Three will depart this world. Be ready. The mighty Dragos will once again rule the elemental realms of this world as they did in the days of your ancient ancestors."

Ilkay did not believe earthly beings, even dragons, could displace her gods, luminous and certain in their heavenly realm. But she shuddered at the rock-eagle's pronouncement. *She speaks of chaos. Of the fight against the Shadow mentioned in the prophecies of Vas O'Nai.*

44

Repeating Vahgrin's sentiment, Ilkay asked herself, "What have I done?"

CHAPTER 5

The magical wavering window before them revealed Ilkay's homeland. Still, she would have to journey, if only briefly, through Vay'Nada's realm to reach it. She closed her eyes and prayed to the Three to protect her.

Though her time in the Shadow's realm was brief, Ilkay experienced a world without the Brothers' light. *I hope never to live that again.* She had to shake off the profound sadness induced by time in Vay'Nada's lair. *I must be ready for any tricks these Vay'Nada spawn try.*

With an agility that belied his size, Vahgrin swooped down and landed, though not directly inside the walls of Ilkay's village. She glimpsed the walls in the distance as she eagerly scrambled from his back on jelly legs. *Less than an hour's walk. Thank the Three, Vahgrin does not seem inclined to feast on my loved ones or burn my home.*

The rock eagle, still perched on Vahgrin's back, said, "Use your dragon tear wisely, young one. And count yourself a fortunate soul, for you have witnessed the rebirth of a living god and survived to tell the tale. And tell it you must. We, sisters of the Dragos, want your kind to know we live still, and our gods will be reborn."

What is she squawking about? Dragons are fearsome, but they are not gods. Still, Ilkay shuddered at the idea that Vahgrin was not the only dragon alive. Ilkay wanted to set the crone straight—to stand up for the Three and the elemental gods as the true gods. But she checked herself. *I am still within Vahgrin's ability to snatch and make into a meal. Besides, if I get killed, who will warn the others?*

"I will tell the others what you said. This I swear," Ilkay said.

The rock-eagle nodded once, then said, "Ashtanga Volenex, Vahgrin."

Vahgrin gave Ilkay one last side-eye glare, then took wing. Again, Ilkay smelled sky-fire, and a terrible wound opened in the heavens. Then Vahgrin and the rock eagle vanished. *It's like they never existed.*

Ilkay's legs were still unsteady, and her heart pounded like a thukna herd. She should have been sweating profusely in the now mid-day light of the Brothers, but her skin was cold, her mouth dry. *When did I last eat or drink?* It could have been only minutes ago, but it felt like years since she'd enjoyed a proper meal. *I must make haste before I falter.*

Seeing the comforting walls of her village in the distance gave her strength. *Cling to life, Father. I will be home soon.*

Ilkay ran, though she had no strength left to run. Hope fueled her. It was all she had left.

She arrived at the gates of her village ragged, her clothes tattered from relentless wind and stinging sand. With Ilkay's keffla wrapped tightly and only her eyes visible, the wall's watchers did not recognize her. The gates did not open as she approached.

"We do not allow pesha here," a guard said.

Ilkay tore the keffla from her head and held up the sac holding Vahgrin's precious tear. "I am Ilkay, and I return with the medicine Hishnari sent me to retrieve."

The other guard, a woman, hollered down. "Open the gates. It is Ilkay. Open the gates for Ilkay."

The wide wood gates creaked open, and several people rushed toward Ilkay. Seeing friendly faces and knowing she was safely home, the wellspring of energy that had fueled her quest finally gave way to the exhaustion she had held at bay. Ilkay's knees gave out, and she collapsed into the first pair of sturdy arms to reach her.

"Get Hishnari. Tell her I have returned with what she requires."

Ilkay closed her eyes and fell into the black emptiness of a dreamless sleep.

When Ilkay woke, she was in her own bed. Brother Hiyadi had gone to his daily rest, and only Niyadi's pale light shone through her window. She'd been washed and dressed in her sleeping linen. Ilkay pushed up and sprang to her feet. Though her body ached with a weariness she feared may never recede, she did not have the luxury of rest. *I must see if my bargain with Vay'Nada's spawn at least saved my father.*

Her father and brother usually shared a sleeping platform in the main room of their small home. Her younger brother, though, was sleeping on a reed mat near the cookfire. On the sleeping platform, her father was still and quiet. As she approached, though, she saw the gentle rise and fall of his chest.

Ilkay let out an audible sigh of relief. *Thank the Three.*

She knelt by his side, her hand on his wrinkled one in repose on his belly. The lines at the sides of his eyes seemed deeper, his skin more sallow than she'd remembered.

Ilkay put her ear to his chest. Before she left, she could hear his breath rattle inside him, and he coughed and sputtered as he tried to get enough air. Now, though, his breath did not sound caged.

"Are you free of the curse, Father?" she whispered.

She had not expected an answer. From the shadows, Hishnari spoke. "Only time will tell."

Intent only on seeing to her father, Ilkay had not seen Hishnari huddled on a stool at his feet. "So, you crafted the elixir? And you gave it to him already?"

Hishnari nodded. "I had it all prepared, waiting for the one ingredient only you could provide."

"But you didn't know what the ingredient would be. How could you know what you needed to balance the tonic?"

The old woman rose and shed the quilt covering her lap. "You truly believe I would send you to Volenex if I had not known precisely what I needed you to find?"

Something about the old Bruxia changed, subtle but unmistakable. Hishnari's eyes became darker, her skin pale. A sick feeling washed over Ilkay, and she swallowed to keep the rising bile down.

Hishnari moved closer, her eyes beady and alight with fervor. "Yes, you see it now, don't you?" The crone nodded and swooped her head closer. "A Dragos Sister, yes. I knew what cure he required because I am the one who laid the curse."

Ilkay stepped back, wishing she couldn't smell the now familiar scent of wet feathers and rot that permeated the air around Nixan. Her head swam, and cold sweat beaded on her forehead. "No. This cannot be. You are our Bruxia. Like a grandmother to me and the village. You cannot be one of—"

"One of the Dragos? Oh yes. We, sisters of the Dragos, are patient. Waiting. Watching for signs. Preparing. Searching for the one who would aid us in our quest to raise the mighty Dragos di Vatra. Our lord and father, Vahgrin." Spittle shone on her bottom lip, and her eyes were dangerous with a fanatic's fervor.

Tears spilled from Ilkay's eyes. "You filthy Vay'Nada spawn. Trickster and devil. Get out of our house. Go then to Volenex. I watched Vahgrin devour two of your sisters whole. With any luck, he made a feast of the rest of your kind. Go to him and rid our village of your foul stench."

Ilkay would never have spoken to Bruxia Hishnari that way. Disrespect for a revered elder brought shame to a household. *But this Nixan is no Bruxia, and I owe no respect to Vay'Nada's spawn.*

Hishnari grinned, revealing the oily, brackish film like the old rock-eagle. "If you returned with his tear, that means Vahgrin succumbed to the rend. And he will not harm me or my sisters."

She threw off her shawl. "But I cannot say the same for others of your kind. He slept over a thousand years. He will be hungry."

"You nurtured me like a grandchild all these years, and the rock-eagle let me live only so you can feed me and my kin to your pet dragon?" Ilkay shook with rage and worry.

The Nixan cackled. "We are Vay'Nada's children, but we are not without honor. You will survive, Ilkay, because you bear the feather of promise. Keep it with you always, and we will spare you and your kin."

Ilkay had forgotten the single mottled feather she'd tucked in her pack. She assumed it was still there.

"Spread word of the glorious news, Ilkay. The Dragos has arisen! Soon, people will witness his power." She morphed then, as Ilkay had seen the women at Volenex do. Hishnari became a giant falcon, and she dropped a single feather of promise to the ground at Ilkay's feet. The falcon uttered a piercing cry. It hopped to the center of the room and flew out of the smoke hole. The bird disappeared into the night lit by Niyadi's pale light.

Ilkay's younger brother, Javron, stumbled to her side, wiping sleep from his eyes. "What was that?" He lifted the single, oversized falcon feather and handed it to her.

She held the feather in her trembling hand. "It was a harbinger, Javron."

He looked at her with puzzlement. "Harbinger?"

He is too young yet to fully understand what this means. Ilkay glanced at her father, still in repose but alive, and she mustered a weak smile for Javron. "What is important is that father lives." She took Javron's hand. "*We* live, brother. Let us thank the Three for that."

Javron wrapped his arms around her. "Father will live." He looked up at her with a wide, joyful smile and expectant eyes.

Ilkay could not bring herself to tell him that their world—life as they had known it—would soon end. And she could not reveal that in her zeal to save their father, she had unwittingly aided Vay'Nada in his quest to bring Shadow to their world.

Let us enjoy the love of our kin today, for the Shadow's beast may devour us tomorrow.

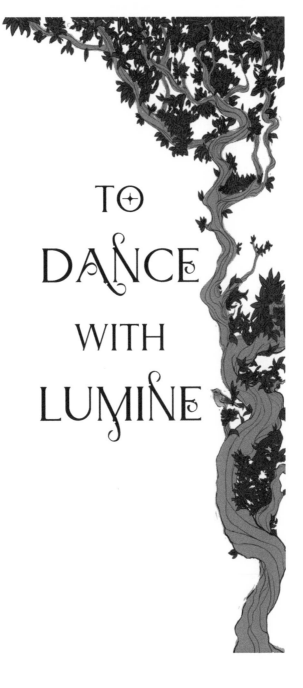

TO

DANCE

WITH

LUMINE

TO DANCE WITH LUMINE

F rom formless night,
   Terrible in its endless doom,
Doj'Badi, our Great Father,
Bellowed into the Void.

"Is solitude to be,
Fate's sole cruel gift to me?
Is eternal dust,
All I will ever see?"

The firmament thundered,
Infinite night shunted,
As a bold and luminous beauty
Tore the nether veil.

Radiant, she twirled and danced,
Gleaming dust in her wake.
Alone no more, they swirled and embraced,
Love taking hold.

In his clumsy clutches,
Doj'Badi gathered stones to forge a ring.
"For Doj'Madi to wear,
And bind our love for eternity."

His plan unknown, she did not choose,
To don his token of love.
Doj'Madi, our Great Mother,
Devoured the ring instead.

Still intent to bind her eternal affection,
Doj'Badi fashioned a necklace,
With stars this time instead.

Shimmering morsels, too glorious to ignore,
Doj'Madi swallowed the necklace whole,
And asked for more.

Swirling dust and creamy clouds,
Surrounded Great Father then.
He tugged and tore until endless stars,
Lit the plane ahead.

Still unsated, Doj'Madi gobbled,
Until her gullet was full,
And no more stars could she devour.

Swollen and sated, Great Mother cried,
"No more!"
And from her mouth radiated,
The boundless light of her firstborn.

Great Father pulled, and Madi coughed,
Until Hiyadi's light shone forth.
In the firmament, she placed this new Soli,
And Doj'Badi was much pleased.

Their new son twirled and gathered,
Swirling dust to his tiny form.
Until he was large and bright,
And the parents were alone no more.

They passed contented eons, did the three,
Until one day, Badi observed,
"Hiyadi plays no more."

"The sweet angel of light you bore,
Casts a shadow of gloom these days."

Doj'Madi, swift in her reply,
"Then a brother shall we create."

Great Father fashioned a new ring,
For our Great Madi to devour.
And she sucked it dry like a dog,
Licking for marrow.

Again, she glowed and, this time, pulled,
From way down deep inside,
A wee soli, bright and cheerful,
And she named him Niyadi.

At last, Hiyadi brightened,
A shadow he cast no more.
With a brother, he played and chased,
As he teased, "Catch me if you can!"

After his elder brother, wee Niyadi dashed.
But Hiyadi's girth was his undoing,
His little brother won every race.

Though Hiyadi never won a match,
He had the upper hand.
Though Hiyadi was slow and plump,
His beastly form triumphed.

For as he spun by Niyadi to provoke,
His plump form greedily pulled,
Dust and light from wee Niyadi.

The little brother tried with all his might,
To right himself and gain control.
But he wobbled and remained unsteady,
His racing days behind.

The Brothers, at once best friends,
Now locked in a battle that neither could win.

Great Mother and Father still had work to do,
To fill the cosmos with light.
So, they left their sons to live a discontented truce,
They bade the Brothers care for one another,
And promised, "We will be at your side again."

Many eons passed this way,
Two brothers with only the other.
'Til one day, Madi's last tear,
Formed a luminous orb.

Immediately smitten by her aloof beauty,
Hiyadi clambered for her favor.
He whispered to the fickle winds,
Her gentle name, Lumine.

Juka, the Trickster, heard his plea,
And delighted in a ruse.
"Deliver the message? Of course," she said.
But she went to Little Brother instead.

A gentle breeze tickled at Lumine's ear,
A welcome change she cherished.
She heard but a single name, "Niyadi,"
And she did not tarry.

Lumine had longed to meet a celestial friend,
To warm her face and end the ceaseless night.
She answered Niyadi's supposed affections,
And bid wee Niyadi be her only love.

Niyadi was surprised, of course,
But not because he was not smitten.
He had seen Lumine, but stayed away,
As shyness kept him hidden.

"She called for me?" he asked Juka.
"Are you certain I am the one?"

"Yours is the only name, the fair one doth call."

Niyadi stalled no longer.
He hurried to her side.
And in a dance, the two did lock for a thousand
years and more.

Together, they watched as on the world below,
Abundant life arose and flourished,
Dead and lifeless was Menauld no more.

While Niyadi and Lumine danced,
And delighted in the life come to Menauld,
Hiyadi fumed and resumed his feud,
With Niyadi, after all.

"How dare he flaunt his passions so!
'Tis unseemly and will not do."
Hiyadi's rage knew no bounds,
He flung wee Niyadi to the outer realms.

Niyadi hurtled to the land of the Shadow,
Where no stars or other bars could stall his
descent.

With Niyadi gone, and Lumine alone,
Hiyadi made his move.
He begged for favor from the fair moon,
For a dance like his brother had got.

"Now, Lumine, with little Brother away,
You belong to me.
Favor me with your dance,
For all eternity."

Lumine's heart, heavy with loss,
She spurned Hiyadi's affection.

To make her point,
And so none could debate her,
She cursed the soli for all to hear,
The Fates did take note.

"Awake by night, to the Shadow by day,
My face never more will you see.
I'll wait and hope for Niyadi's love,
For all eternity."

And so it was, the Three were split,
Lumine's promise held to bear.

Yet no despair should you hold,
Not all is lost!
For wee Niyadi, brother fair,
His love for Lumine never given up.

Boundless affection swelled his heart,
Lumine's grace he did not forget.
It warmed his nights and fueled his quest,
To escape the cage of the Void's firmament.

To dance once more at Lumine's side,
Wee Niyadi rejoiced.

The two are together, above us locked,
In a dance of eternal bliss.
Known as the soli that never sleeps,
Niyadi yearns still for her kiss.

By day, he sprints from Hiyadi's wrath,
And by night, he rests in Lumine's arms.
Her heart to the wee Brother stays true,
Resisting forever Hiyadi's charms.

—from ECHOS OF THE BEGINNING, 1st Era.
Credited to Hiz'Li'naj di Nari, Cleric of the First
Temple of Lumine (nka Val'Enara)

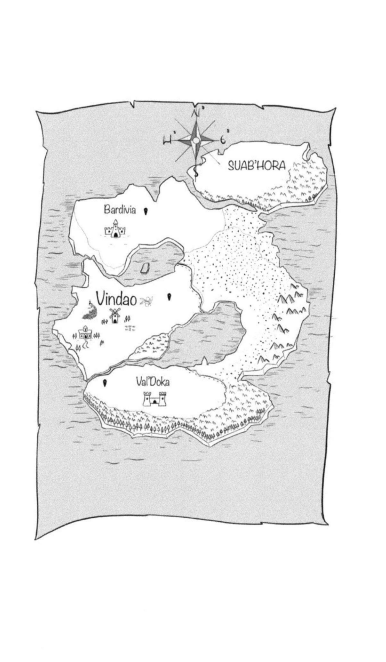

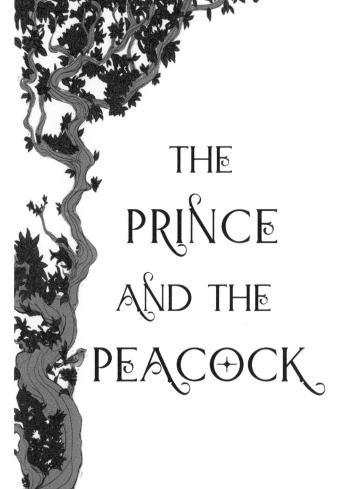

THE
PRINCE
AND THE
PEACOCK

CHAPTER I

The Brothers high in the sky, Prince Vinati woke from his early afternoon nap when the boat ceased swaying. The Prince's ever-present companion Amantu, his pet peacock, fluffed his feathers and squawked disapproval at being roused.

"I agree with you, Amantu," the Prince said. "I did not order you to cease rowing. What say you, Lorencio?"

"'Pologies, my Prince. But you might want to refresh before you greet—her." Lorencio pointed the butt of his oar across the pond. A gondola approached swiftly from the west.

Benigia, Curia Regina to the Queen, sat perched at the bow of the gondola. The breeze lifted her purple scarf and flapped it like a wagging tongue. Her thin lips were pulled tight, and her dark brows pinched.

Prince Vinati rose and brushed the dust from his golden silk pants. Amantu continued screeching, his strident voice contrasting his multicolored plumage's ornate beauty.

Vinati stroked Amantu's feathered head. "Be still, Amantu." The bird quieted at his soft touch and calming voice. "The bearer of our Queen Mother's tidings approaches."

Lorencio coughed and, when he had Vinati's attention, nodded toward the Prince's tunic. Vinati had removed it to allow Hiyadi's light to warm his golden-brown skin. He shook out the teal-blue silk and quickly donned it. He sat up straight, ran a hand through his long, black hair, and hitched an arm around Amantu's plump body.

The oarsman of Benigia's boat sidled up to the prince's gondola so the two members of King Nérandu's court could speak. Benigia wasted no time with niceties. "Come, Vin. You are required at court at once." Though she had never been the prince's caretaker, she spoke to him in the tone of a scolding nanny.

And truth be told, she speaks to nearly everyone in that tone.

Prince Vinati bristled at her use of the nickname used by his parents and closest friends. He could have let it go, but her interruption of his planned afternoon of basking in Hiyadi's light with Amantu had soured his mood.

But before Vinati could correct Benigia, Lorencio said, "You mean Prince Vinati?"

Benigia's cheeks colored, and she narrowed her eyes at Lorencio. "Mind your station. I need no correction from a mere oarsman." She sneered at Lorencio.

"Apparently, you do. And I am Prince Vinati's Curia Principa, or have you forgotten?" Lorencio said.

Despite Lorencio having no qualifications to counsel a king-in-waiting, Prince Vinati had named Lorencio his chief advisor. Since Vinati's only duties were waiting and watching, Lorencio's new title as Curia Principa meant little more than being the prince's oarsman and valet.

Benigia laughed and was about to speak, but Vinati cut her off sternly. "Enough. You two get your feathers ruffled more easily than Amantu. You paddled here for a reason, Benigia. What does Queen Gosea demand of me this afternoon?"

Benigia retrieved a scroll from a slim pocket inside the bell-shaped sleeve of her tunic. "This is the list of courtesans attending this afternoon's Presentment of the Vine."

She held the scroll out to Vinati, but he hesitated to take it. Vin knew the names on the list belonged to the most elegant, talented, and intelligent women in Bardivia. Vinati had no desire to make small talk with a parade of women whose sole goal was to wed a man they barely knew. He would have preferred a lecture on proper vine pruning.

His mother's Curia coughed and brandished the scroll. "It will not bite."

Vinati sighed and took the scroll. He unfurled the reed-pulp paper. The names of seven women he'd never met became a sea of ink. Feeling dizzy, Vinati teetered. Lorencio's firm hand on his arm shored him up.

"Oh, poor Prince." Benigia put the back of her hand to her forehead, pretending to be faint. "He must endure the company of the seven most refined women in all the Vindaô Province. Whatever shall he do?"

Benigia's mocking reflected the general response he received to his display of any reluctance to partake in the choreography required of him to choose a wife.

Vinati stroked Amantu's feathers, which calmed him enough to cease his dizziness. If only he could express his feelings to his mother. To tell the Queen that he preferred a simple life without the realm's weight on his shoulders. He yearned to be a farmer or vintner. He wanted to spend his days in the field with his peacock at his side and his nights with a cup of wine by the fire, curled next to Amantu.

But he would take his father's place as ruler. And he'd father the next generation of rulers to intermediate between the land and the gods. *A burden for which I did not pray and do not cherish.*

Vinati rolled the scroll and thrust it toward Benigia. "Return this to Queen Gosea with this message. I do not intend to pluck a bride from a stable of maidens like a cook choosing a goose for feasting day."

Benigia's eyes grew dark. She pursed her lips, ready to speak.

But Vinati raised his hand to halt her words. "Do not spout old superstitions to sway me. The gods have more to do than squander their concern over whether I take a wife and produce heirs for Bardivia. The fields will not go fallow. The vines will not wither if I remain a carefree prince, untethered to a hen."

"Like all Bardivia's kings that precede you, you must follow the customs. Remember your lessons of Prince Ignoti, your great-great grandsire?"

Vinati tsked. "And yet here I am." He gestured to the verdant hills surrounding the pond. "And here Bardivia stands. They built her foundations on stronger stuff than one man's soul."

Lorencio poured Caldovian red into a goblet and handed it to the prince. Vinati drank heartily, and the wine made him bold enough to suggest a plan for Bardivia's future. He'd hatched the idea recently after he'd reached the bottom of his cup at the Beak's Breath Inn.

"Besides, Horence will be of age in a year or two. He will happily pluck a prized maiden and make many heirs." Vinati drank more wine and hiccupped. "Both legitimate and illegitimate." He laughed. "Plenty of heirs to mediate with the gods." He gestured, spilling wine into the pond. "Worry not, Benigia. Horence has seed enough for two princes."

Benigia gasped. "Mind your tongue, Prince."

Lorencio refilled Vinati's cup, and the prince drank deeply. "Or what?" He slurred his words. "Will you run like a startled fawn and tattle on me to my mother?"

Amantu screeched as if to punctuate the Prince's question.

"And you." Benigia pointed a thin finger at Lorencio. "He may have named you Curia, but you are a servant. Do not forget yourself. Enabling his lascivious behavior and propensity to shirk his duties only to romp with this—" She pointed at Amantu. "This... feathered nuisance. It does you no credit in the Queen's eyes."

Lorencio re-corked the wine flask.

"Come now, Lorencio. Do not listen to this featherless old hen." Vinati heralded Benigia with his goblet, more wine spilling into the pond between their boats. "Run to Queen Gosea with haste. Give her my regards and answer. She will want to create an excuse for my absence so that everything appears in order." He drained the goblet and muttered, "The gods know how much appearances mean to her."

Benigia, seeing she was unlikely to sway the young liege, tucked the scroll back into her sleeve and ordered her oarsman to return to the palace. She called back, "Mark well my words, young prince. The fertility of the land is bound to your folly as surely as Lumine's fate is tied to the dance of the Brothers. Should you deny planting your seed in fertile ground, the fields will go fallow, and the vines wither. And you and your kin will lose the realm."

Prince Vinati had heard such dire prophecies before. But now, as in the past, the warnings fell on deaf ears. He held up his cup. "To Lumine." He glanced up at the Brothers high overhead, sipped, and added, "And to Brotherly love."

CHAPTER 2

T rue to his word, Prince Vinati did not attend the Presentment of the Vine. The entire city-state of Bardivia was filled with idle chatter about the Prince's absence at the year's most attended festival. Tongues wagged about his failure to court a single courtesan, hand-chosen by the Queen and her advisors.

The Prince's failure to court a bride made it appear that he thought himself too good for the daughters of Bardivia. A few noted the Prince's proclivity to spend his days and nights in the constant company of Amantu. The rumors that he preferred his feathered friend to a woman's arms made people snicker behind his back. People began referring to him as the Prince of the Peacocks.

These observations were not lost on Vinati's mother. She was Queen first and duty-bound to protect the realm. Like any mother, Queen Gosea hoped for her son's happiness. But she put the good of the kingdom before Vinati's desires. She had not been wildly in love with King Nérandu before marriage, yet they became friends and partners in ruling the realm. Queen Gosea often said, "Fondness grows with familiarity."

Though Vinati's words to Benigia had been brash (emboldened by the wine, no doubt), he feared facing the Queen. To avoid whispers of courtesans behind their silk fans and his mother's increasingly harsh entreaties, Vinati escaped the stifling city. He retreated to the countryside's vineyards.

Masquerading as a farmer's son, Vinati donned the rough-spun, knee-length linen breeches, linen shirt, and sandals of a commoner. Vinati left even his Curia, Lorencio, behind in Bardivia. With only his feathered friend Amantu at his side, Vin pretended to be a young man named Domini and roamed the countryside.

He made his way northeast and supported himself by picking grapes, carrying fruit baskets, and tilling furrows. At first, his soft, clean hands nearly revealed his identity. But after a few weeks, his hands calloused, and his nails took on the ground-in-dirt patina of a life lived by nature's clock.

Vinati roamed the countryside as a day laborer for weeks. Eventually, he entered the estate of an up-and-coming winemaker, Ser Nephil. Though no one had realized Vinati's true identity for weeks, Nephil recognized him immediately but hired him anyway.

"Who am I to question a young man's right to experience the world?" Ser Nephil asked. "Even a prince may scatter wild seed before he gets yoked to the crown."

"This is no folly, good Ser," Vinati said. "I am in earnest. I do not intend to become king. I prefer a simpler life. Perhaps as a purveyor of the vine, like you."

"Simple, hey?" Ser Nephil harrumphed and whispered, "Shows what he knows about winemaking." Nephil wiped his brow with a sweat-stained hanky. "It may be fine for *you* to give up the throne. But who will manage the realm?"

"That duty will fall to my younger brother, Horence."

Nephil laughed heartily.

"Here, here," Vinati said. "That is my brother you laugh at, Ser."

Nephil wiped a tear from his eye and calmed his laughter. "Forgive me, half-liege. May I speak frankly?"

Vinati nodded. "Speak plainly, Ser, and tell me what caused your mirth."

"It is—well, everyone knows about Horence's ways."

Vin held little love for his brother. But he could not ignore an insult directed at his kin. Heat rose up his neck. "What does *everyone* know, Ser Nephil?"

Nephil's smile was gone. "I mean you no offense, Prince Vinati. Despite your recent disappearance and rumors, you are well-liked by the people of Bardivia. By the whole of the Vindaô Province. Folks cut you slack on account of your youth. Sowing seeds and all that. They say you have your mother's grace and beauty and your father's wit and kindly demeanor."

Servants and court denizens frequently showered the prince with praise, but he had never received a compliment from someone not on the palace payroll. Prince Vinati's throat tightened with emotion. "Kind words, good Ser." He cleared his throat. "Thank you for the praise. But what do people say of Horence?"

"To put it simply, Horence is—not you. Folks say Horence indulges in all manner of vice and extravagance. People talk of seeing him drowning in his cups. They say he spends his time tangled in the skirts of this lady or that. The good folks of the Vindaô fear he lacks our dear King Nérandu's wisdom or our treasured Queen Gosea's grace."

Prince Vinati knew Nephil's criticism of Horence to be true. Horence had no mind for history or ledgers. And he had the patience of a starving dog near fresh meat.

Though true, the good vintner's words angered Vinati anyway. He was cross at the situation, not the vintner. *Is there no peace from duty's incessant drum beating at me?*

Rather than argue against what Ser Nephil said about Horence, Vinati rolled the legs of his breeches and stepped into the vat of grapes. He stomped and mashed the fruit into a pulp, sweat beading on his forehead.

Amantu, perhaps sensing Vinati's agitation, flapped and screeched.

"The bird is telling you to slow up, my Prince," Nephil said. He poured another bucket of grapes into the large wood vat. "I cannot keep up with your furious maceration."

Prince Vinati wiped his brow with a billowy sleeve but did not slow his pace. "Please, Ser Nephil, I am not a prince here. I am Domini, apprentice to a master of the vine." He flashed a glowing white smile, his deep brown eyes alight.

For a time, there was only the sound of grapes squishing and juice splashing into large clay jars. Sweat soaked Prince Vinati's linen shirt. His legs felt like lead, but he reveled in the beauty of the humble task. No courtesans chattering to him about mundane matters or gossip. No court advisors grilled him on the intricacies of the Bardivian merchant class and their favored trading partners among the great Mājas of Partha. Here, he did not have to meet his father's gaze and wither beneath his mother's reproaches.

Sweat dripped from his brow, mixing with the sweet nectar of the sacred fruit. Vinati continued stomping and pondered Ser Nephil's words. Though what Nephil said of Horence was accurate, Bardivia's gossips failed to consider that King Nérandu was not old. He would manage Bardivia for many years. And the king employed capable advisors. *They will care for the realm even if something happens to Father.*

After aiding Ser Nephil with his harvest, Vinati searched for a farm to call his own. He had gathered enough knowledge from Nephil that he was confident he could grow vines to make wine. "I will create a life for myself and Amantu, far from the headaches of the King's court."

CHAPTER 3

T hough winter in the Vindaô is brief, the
fallow season gave Prince Vinati time to
find an appropriate residence. He and
Amantu moved into a small, abandoned
cottage at the northern edge of Bardivia's reach.
Once a thriving olive grove, the farm had
suffered neglect.

"We will bring it back to its former glory,"
Prince Vinati declared.

Amantu did not disagree. He stood at
Vinati's side, even though he had given up a
life of ease at the palace. In the palace's Peacock
Garden, Amantu spent his days plucking tasty
insects from the fertile ground and bedding
down in a toasty bed at Vinati's side. Since
leaving Ser Nephil's verdant farm, Amantu
survived on meager rations and spent nights in
a frigid cottage with thread-bare blankets.

"If only human companions were so loyal," Vinati said.

Amantu snuggled his head into Vinati's palm and fluffed his feathers. The peacock was content with the prince's gentle touch as full payment for his loyalty.

By day, Vinati cleaned and repaired the cottage and cleared the groves of dead wood. By night, he played flute by the fire and laughed at Amantu's preening and antics. Without court life's headaches, Vinati was truly happy for the first time.

The short winter gave way to an early spring. Secluded by anonymity at the far reaches of Bardivia's realm, Prince Vinati heard nothing of the court or political affairs.

He planted a small garden and vines gifted to him by Nephil. Vinati followed Ser Nephil's instructions to the letter, but despite the vine stock being the best in Bardivia, the vines failed within a few weeks. The spring brought heat like mid-summer but no rain. Pests abounded and ate the tender garden shoots. Within days, ravenous insects devoured Prince Vinati's efforts.

Assuming he had made a mistake while planting, Vinati ventured to the next farm south. Upon cresting the hill and looking down at his neighbor's steading, he stopped cold.

Vinati and Amantu had passed this farm only a few months ago. They'd seen rows of vibrant olive trees, healthy vines, and staked hops bushes. Early winter lettuces had glistened in the midday sun, deep green and covered in dew.

Now, pests had eaten the lettuce leaves into lace. Drought withered the hops bushes and made the grapevines desiccated sticks. Trees should have been springing alive with new buds but were barren.

Vinati ventured to the main house and knocked. When no one answered, he wandered to the barn and outdoor animal pens.

He found the farmer by the chicken coop. The man sat on a stool, his head in his hands. Dead chickens surrounded him, their eyes glazed over, flies already buzzing.

Vinati's voice was a whisper. "What happened here?"

The man's eyes were red and watery. His tone held a bitter edge. "It's a blight like in the prophecies of Vas O'Nai. His teachings warn us not to anger the gods. We angered 'em good, yes, we have. And this is our punishment. No living thing will survive it." The farmer wiped his eyes on his dirty sleeve. "I blame King Nérandu." The man shook his head. "Yep, it's all the King's fault."

Though the Prince often disagreed with his father and resented the King's relentless pressure to fulfill his courtly duties, Prince Vinati loved his father well. Hearing someone speak so angrily of his beloved father raised his ire.

"Now see here, man. You should not speak of our King that way. He is a dedicated servant of the people. How can you blame your misfortune on him?"

The man spat at the dusty soil. "Fah. If he was dedicated, he'd 'ave raised a better son to take his place. A Prince with honor. Instead, he's got one cowardly son who runs to gods-know-where and another that cares only for drink and women." Hot tears sprang to the man's eyes. "My dutiful sons had to leave to find food. I can't even care for my family now because of that selfish Prince Vinati." To punctuate his displeasure, the man spit again.

Prince Vinati's stomach roiled, and he feared his meager breakfast would come back up. His breaths were shallow, and his head spun. The Prince wiped his brow and neck and tried to calm himself lest the man wonder at his odd behavior.

Prince Vinati had assumed the talk of how the King and royal family intermediate between the gods and man was a myth. *A convenient story created to yoke men like me to duty.* He had never believed it could be true.

Is it possible that I am, in fact, to blame for this poor man's misfortune? The Prince gazed at the withered vines, dead fowl, and fallow fields. Though he had taken an extended break from his court duties, nothing had changed. His father, the King, still sat on the Vinland Throne in Bardivia. *So long as he lives, the gods have their intermediary. Me and my family cannot be to blame for this.*

"I shall pray to the Brothers on your behalf, Ser, but I disagree that our good King is to blame. So long as he sits on the Vinland Throne, we cannot lay blame for a blight at his feet."

The farmer squinted up at Vinati. Shading his eyes from the sun, he fully took Vinati in for the first time. "You don't look addle-brained. Where have you been? Ain't you heard?"

Vinati sensed he had not heard the worst this man would say. The Prince's heart raced. "Heard what?"

The man rose and gazed up into Vinati's eyes. "The King has taken ill. They say he's dying, and the land is dying with him."

Blackness played at the edges of Prince Vinati's vision. The ground swirled, and his chest tightened. Amantu squawked, and the farmer put a hand on Vinati's arm.

"Are you all right, man? You look like you saw an apparition."

Prince Vinati felt as though he had seen a spirit. A vision of his father's ghost intermingled with a future he now knew he would never have. He shook his head to clear his thoughts and took a deep, calming breath.

The Prince ran from the farmer's grave misfortune. Vinati could not help what befell this man or others. Though knowledge of his part in people's misery would leave a lifelong scar, he thought of only one person now.

The farmer called to him, but Vinati was too busy praying to understand the man's words.

Hear me, Wopang. Be with my father now and wrap him in your loving vines.

He spoke aloud and hoped Juka carried his words as a whisper in his father's ear. "Be strong, father. Your prince soon returns."

CHAPTER 4

With Amantu tucked under his arm, Prince Vinati ran south on dusty roads. After several hours, he spied a wagon and called the driver. "Ho, wait for a weary traveler."

To his surprise, the wagon driver halted. Dozens of wine casks weighed down the wagon. *He must be going to Bardivia to sell his wine.*

When the Prince caught up to the wagon, he sighed with relief. The driver was none other than Ser Nephil. His hands on his knees, Vinati panted and said, "By the grace of the Three, Ser Nephil, am I ever glad to see you."

Nephil held out a hand to help him up. "I assume you are headed to Bardivia?"

Vinati put Amantu atop a cask and sat on the narrow bench next to Nephil. "I am."

Under his breath, Nephil muttered, "About time."

Prince Vinati pretended he had not heard the recrimination. He cleared his parched throat. "You're hauling nearly your entire cellar to Bardivia. Why?"

Nephil gave him a sidelong glance. His jaw was set, his lips a thin line. "'Cause the wells are running dry, my Prince." He clipped his words. "The wells await rains that have not come. The people are thirsty. Until Lumine blesses us with her waters, maybe my wine and juice from the last harvest will keep them alive. For now."

Prince Vinati had no words. He apologized as he'd begun believing the realm's misfortune lay on his shoulders.

Ser Nephil only shook his head in response. "I want to blame it all on you. Truth be told, the fault is not yours alone. I could have—*should have*—sent you back home. If I had—"

"If you had sent me away, I would have wandered onto another vintner's land." He put a hand on Nephil's arm. "Do not take the blame on yourself, Ser Nephil. There is nothing you could have done to prevent this calamity."

They rode through the night, not stopping to rest. Vinati took the reins when Nephil nodded off. The men spoke no further and rode in uncomfortable silence. They arrived the next day when the Brothers were both high overhead.

When the wagon first entered Bardivia's gates, laughing children chased after it. People cheered Ser Nephil for bringing them the potentially life-saving elixir.

But as they made their way closer to the palatial section of the city, people recognized Prince Vinati despite his commoner's garb. Boos and jeers directed at the Prince replaced the prior good cheer directed at Ser Nephil.

"Make haste to the palace, Ser Nephil. I fear if we linger long outside the palace walls, these good folk will tear me apart."

Nephil did not answer but tsked and gave his horses a "Yaw!"

Expecting the cargo, the gates of the palace grounds opened for Ser Nephil. The guards smiled broadly, and a few even saluted, not because they recognized the prince but because the sight of the wine casks lifted their spirits.

Ser Nephil made his way to the cargo unloading area at the back of the palace, but Prince Vinati and Amantu jumped from the ambling cart as they neared the front gardens.

"May the Three bless you, Ser Nephil, and my thanks to you many times over." He waved and added, "And I promise. I will make this right."

Nephil shook his head and denied the prince a cheerful reply. He muttered, "Make it right if you can. But sometimes you can't set straight something that's too far broken."

Vinati approached the palace, and the guards stepped before the doors to block his entry. One of them tsked. The other said, "Go back down the hill, pesha. The Queen's got no more food to hand out today."

Prince Vinati removed his vintner's cap and let loose his braid, allowing his long black hair to flow over his shoulders. He stood tall and took on the "I am your better" attitude honed into him by his mother.

He spoke with the haughty air she'd also taught him, his voice tinged with imperious anger. "You would deny entry to your Prince?"

The two guards immediately recognized him. They stepped aside, their eyes downcast.

"'Pologies, my Prince."

They showed deference, but there was no affection in their greeting, as Prince Vinati was accustomed to. He did not linger for more apologies, though. Vinati sprinted to his father's solar.

Benigia, his mother's Curia, stopped him in the vestibule of his father's private wing. "Where do you think you are going?"

He panted and, though winded, said, "Step aside, Benigia. I have no time for trading barbs with you today. I must see my father."

He moved to step around her, but she shoved an ample hip out to block his entry. Her eyes wide and bleary with tears, she entreated him. "You ignored your tutors and my warnings. You even disregarded the teachings of the Kentaros brought from Val'Doka to instruct you on the complex weave of our relationship with the gods. But you would not hear it. And now?" Her lower lip trembled.

"I have no time for your reproaches. Where is my mother?"

Benigia sighed and reluctantly stepped to the side, revealing the door. "You will find our dearest Queen inside at your father's side, where she has remained since he took ill. I pray you break her heart no further. You have done enough of that already."

It was, as Benigia said. King Nérandu lay in repose with his mother's head resting on his still hand. Usually sporting smooth cheeks and chin alive with vibrant color, salt-and-pepper grizzle covered the King's face, his color sallow.

Queen Gosea wore a simple linen tunic over linen pants rather than her typical silks. She wore no hair adornments, necklaces, or rings save for the garnet cabochon ring his father placed on the middle finger or her left hand the day they bonded.

Upon hearing someone enter, Queen Gosea said in a thin voice, "I said I want to be alone with him, Benigia."

Prince Vinati stepped lightly toward the bed, his hands clutching at the brim of the hat in his hands. "It is I, Mother. Vinati."

She blinked, eyes rimmed in red and puffy. He had expected her to pile accusations and anger upon him. Instead, his mother poured herself into his arms and wet his shirt with tears. His Queen Mother, always strong, stern, and regal, wept in great swelling sobs.

She might have remained there, but the King's frail voice interrupted. "Come, now. Do not weep, my Queen. I am not dead yet." He tried to laugh, but instead, he gave a choked cough.

Gosea whispered into Vinati's ear. "Go to him. Let him see you one last time."

"One last time." The haunting words made Vinati's stomach feel hollow.

He knelt by his father's bedside and took the King's hands. When he'd left Bardivia, his father had been vibrant and the picture of health and vitality.

But now, his father's hands were like the withered vines of his farm. Vinati smoothed a stray hair from his father's pallid forehead. "I am here, father. It is I, Vinati."

The King's eyes, pupils dilated and groggy from the nys't, searched for Vinati. When he finally landed on Vinati's face, the King smiled wanly. "Where did you go, my boy?"

Before he'd left the confines of the palace walls, his father calling him "boy" would have rankled him. Perhaps it would still had he not looked into the eyes of a dying man. "I had to see the world, father. Forgive me, my King." Vinati wept. "I did not know you were ill. I came as soon as I learned of your condition."

The King squeezed Vinati's hand with what little strength remained. "Shush now, son. We've no time for could-haves and might-have-beens."

Nérandu coughed, and Queen Gosea handed Vinati a cloth to wipe the spittle from the King's lips.

"Listen." The King motioned for Vinati to edge closer. "My illness. It isn't your fault."

Prince Vinati protested, and even Queen Gosea inserted herself to agree with Vinati on the point. But the King cut them both off, his deep bass voice showing some of its prior strength.

"The people will chastise you, rightly, for running from your duties to this land. But my failing, as their King, caused their crops to fail, the vines to wither, and the wells to run dry."

"No, Father. You cannot hold yourself to blame. I ran from my duties like a coward. You are an honorable king."

King Nérandu shook his head. "Honor?" He gave a wry laugh. "I dishonored the gods, not you. Your absence left me bereft and revealed my weakness. I sought comfort in another's arms and broke vows to Doka and my Queen." His eyes welled with tears. "Forgive me, Gosea, if you can. Cast no further blame on your noble son."

Vinati felt his mother step back from the bed. When he looked back at her, Gosea's face had gone ashen, her eyes wide. She dropped her embroidered handkerchief to the floor. "You?" She shook her head. "Oh Nérandu. How could you?"

He shook his head, his eyes pinched tight, tears at the corners reflecting Vinati's visage back to him. The King said, "I am unworthy of you, Gosea." He turned his bleary eyes to Vinati. "But let my faults be a harrowing lesson to you, my son."

The King coughed again. This time, blood tinged his spittle pink. "When you ascend to the throne, to gain the favor of our patron goddess, Doka, you must bind yourself to a woman like the vines are married to the earth.

Together, you will find the joys of a fruitful family, reflecting the land's bounty, and your bounty reverberates to the entire realm.

"Doka locks us in a dance, you see. She gives of herself generously and asks only for this simple thing in return. As King, you are wed to the land, my son, as you are bound to your Queen. Never forget this, as in my hubris I did."

King Nérandu took a deep breath and released a shuddering sigh. The crease on his forehead relaxed, and his eyes softened.

He has released his heart from a heavy burden.

The King squeezed Vinati's hand again. "Promise me, Vin. Make a vow before the great Doj'Madi that you will heed my words. Pray you remain faithful to your Queen as she represents the bounty of Doka's gift."

Vinati had never heard the King's relationship with Doka explained this way before. The King's words rang true to his core, and he made the solemn vow with all his heart.

"I promise you, Father. I will heed your words and choose a queen. And with her, we will restore Doka's blessing to Vindaô."

The King pulled Vinati's hand to his lips and placed a dry kiss. His strength sapped, Nérandu dropped Vinati's hand, and a lone tear rolled down his face. "Forgive me, my Queen, before I journey to the River."

Prince Vinati reached for his mother's hand and joined it with his father's. "The Kentaros taught that Doka does not bestow her blessings of verdant bounty when warring hearts sunder the kingdom. You love this land's people, mother, as well as any queen before you. To restore the land's bounty and Doka's blessings on our people, we must forgive each other."

Queen Gosea's lip trembled as she kissed her husband's brow. "I forgive the King," she said.

Nérandu's chest rose and fell a few more times. Then his light went out of the world. In one hand, Vinati held his father's hand, growing cold and stiff already. His other hand grasped the still vital hand of his mother. Vinati formed a bridge between two realms. Life in one hand. Death and the threat of Vay'Nada's shadow in the other.

As never before, he understood the role he must play in life's grand theater. Vinati left his mother to her grief. He had entered the room a reluctant prince but left a determined king.

CHAPTER 5

B efore being entombed in the Cave of Kings burrowed into the bedrock of Bardivia beneath the palace, King Nérandu laid in state for two days rather than the usual week afforded kings of Bardivia. The Archon from Val'Doka advised Queen Gosea that the realm could not wait for the typical pomp and circumstance.

"Proceed with haste," the Archon said. "Bardivia must crown a new king—and queen—immediately. For the good of the realm."

Prince Vinati had little time to mourn the loss of his father and king. As he donned the long silk pants and laced tunic of his courtly life, he complained to Amantu. "I should be grateful for the brief respite I had from this task." He sighed. "But I would rather be in the

Peacock Garden with you pecking for insects. Instead, I must suffer hours of small talk with women who do not care to know me. They want only to be raised to the dais as queen."

Amantu fluffed his feathers, raised his extraordinary tail, and chittered in agreement.

The Prince patted Amantu's silky head feathers. "At least I will always have you, my friend."

The Prince attended luncheons, teas, and dinners with his mother, all arranged by Curia Benigia. Queen Gosea favored a candidate that everyone agreed was the most graceful, articulate, and beautiful woman in Bardivia. Prince Vinati endeavored to find a spark of attraction for his mother's favored candidate for the queen. But luminous as she was, the woman looked to the Queen for approval rather than Vinati for affection. Like all the courtesans he'd spoken with, none showed interest in meaningful conversation. *Apologies, my Queen, but surely there must be someone who will at least pretend to care for me.*

Prince Vinati turned to Lorencio for his opinion. "What say you, my Curia Principa? If you are to advise me, who do you favor for binding with me?"

Lorencio inclined his head toward a small woman with fiery hair and a spirit to match. Though not the most graceful of the courtesans, she was undoubtedly the loudest. Amantu flapped and squawked whenever she was near.

"Please tell me you will not take your bird's opinion over your Curia's advice," Lorencio said.

Vinati did not have to answer him. Curia Benigia crossed the brash young woman's name off the list and sent her back to her estate in northern Vindaô.

After a week of dancing with strangers and suffering small talk, Vinati demanded an afternoon free to clear his head. He donned the rough-spun knee-length breeches, simple linen shirt, and straw hat of his alter ego, Domini. With his hair braided and his face under the shadow of the wide-brimmed hat, the palace staff assumed he was a gardener, and they ignored him.

Seeking his best friend's company, Vinati finally went to the Peacock Garden. Drought had withered most of Bardivia, but sparse grasses remained in the Peacock Garden.

Since court duties kept the Prince busy, Amantu had spent more time in the garden. The Prince had expected to find his friend sleeping or perhaps pouting without his prince. Instead, he found Amantu displaying his proud feathers for a particular peahen. Amantu was so engrossed in his preening he did not notice the Prince enter the garden.

I should not feel jealous, yet I do.

The Prince left Amantu to his courting. *I suppose he must find a binding partner, as do I. I cannot expect him to live forever alone, shuttled to the side once I have found a bride.*

His mood darkened. The Prince shoved his hands in his pockets. He headed to the garden's back corner swing to sulk in peace. As he neared the rear of the garden, a song lilted in the air.

> Come hither, fair maidens,
> To the vine halls of Bardivia.
>
> Ooh, fee la, fee di do.

Vinati stood behind a large tree and spied a young woman about his age, her hair undone and silk tunic unlaced. She sat on the swing the Prince had been heading toward and scattered seed to pea hens gathered near her feet.

What a lovely singing voice for such a bawdy song. The Prince's curiosity was piqued. *She is dressed as a courtesan. But this fair maiden learned that song in a vine house.*

The woman, unaware she had company, continued the tavern song.

> Bring bosoms fair,
> And flaxen hair,
> And swoon on bended knee.

The woman laughed then, and though she thought herself alone, her cheeks colored crimson. "Mother would show me the rough side of her tongue if she heard me sing such a song," she said aloud.

Prince Vinati put his hand over his mouth to stifle a laugh. *If Queen Gosea heard her sing that song, she'd put the young lady on the next wagon home.*

Vinati ventured toward her.

The woman gasped when she realized she was undone and not alone. She tsked at him. "Yo, there. You should not sneak up on a lady."

Her accent is southern Vindaô from the lands bordering the Lenxofré Forest. She traveled far.

Prince Vinati removed his straw hat and bowed. Using the vernacular of common folk he'd spent the past summer and autumn with, he said, "'Pologies, my lady. I was no'a tryin' to sneak. You were too busy with your song, I 'spose, to hear my approach."

She blushed again. "Yes, well, I 'pologize that you heard it." She began lacing her outer tunic. "A lady isn't 'sposed to sing such songs." She added under her breath, "A damned boring life, I'm guessing."

"What is, ma'am?"

She gestured around them. "This life. Courtly life."

She clearly does not recognize me. Shall I continue with my subterfuge? He had not had such an entertaining conversation since his time on Nephil's farm. He decided not to reveal his identity.

"You're a courtesan, aren't you? I should suppose you are used to courtly life."

She scoffed and patted the seat beside her, inviting him to join her. "Courtly life. Pah." She'd skipped a hole, and the laces of her tunic now bunched oddly. She blew a stray hair from her face. "I am new here. My ma shipped me here like a sack of turnips. I guess the Queen is desperate to find a bride for her son. Even the likes of me, daughter of a Lenxofré senior elder, might bind with her son."

The woman gave up on her laces, laughed, and held out her hand. "Name's Palomisia, but people mostly call me Pali."

She held her hand sideways, not palm down, in the delicate gesture of a courtesan expecting a gentle kiss. Vinati took her hand in his. Pali's palms were soft, but her fingers bore callouses, and her skin was sun-bronzed. Though protocol forced him to kiss many a courtesan's hand, he despised the ritual. Though he had the urge to plant a light kiss on Pali's hand, he shook it as she intended.

His hand still in hers, Pali asked, "So… What is your name?"

Vinati glanced at her and gave her a languid look. "I go by Domini."

They had held onto each other's hands too long to be appropriate. Her cheeks colored again, and she took her hand from his and cleared her throat. "Nice to meet you, Domini."

They sat in awkward but not unpleasant silence for a few moments. Then, they each spoke at the same time.

Pali started with, "Have you worked here…?"

And Prince Vinati spoke over her, saying, "It must be strange."

"What is strange?"

"To be here, I mean. You hope to court a man you have never met? And one you must despise, as most others do now. After what he did."

Pali smoothed her tunic. "Being here is odd, to be sure. I've had precious little training on being a 'lady.' I came out of duty to my family. And I hear the Prince returned for his duty to the land and the people."

"You don't despise the Prince?" *I despise myself for the trouble I wrought.*

"Nah, I don't dislike the fella. I mean, not yet. I haven't even met him." Pali laughed.

Vinati laughed with her. "Give it time. You might well learn to dislike him once you know him."

Pali's eyes widened with excitement. "Wait. Do you know him?" She lightly punched Vinati's arm. "Well, don't hold back, friend. Tell me all about him."

Prince Vinati blushed three shades of crimson and felt sweat beading on his neck. "Oh, I don't know... I mean, I don't want to give you false impressions. I'm just—"

Pali looked disappointed but let go of her line of inquiry. "Ah, that's all right. You don't want to talk badly about your employer. I respect that."

"Look, it's not that I'm saying he's a good guy or bad. I'm just surprised you hold a good opinion of him, unlike most folks around here these days."

Pali threw seed to the hens. "In the south, our young men rove with their pals before settling into a binding. We call them Vine Lads. They roam the countryside, trading labor for their supper." She pantomimed tipping a cup to her lips. "And spend any coin they earn at wine clubs. The Vine Lads learn about the world, sow oats, and expend the last of their youthful folly before settling down."

"That's what they say the Prince was doing."

Pali gave him a sideways stare, appraising him as if anew. "If Prince Vinati had come from the Lenxofré, people would praise rather than pillory him for what he did. Instead, he's yoked by Doka to shite he never wanted." She cast her gaze downwards. "Same as me, I 'spose."

Pali's demeanor had been gay when he happened upon her, but her mood had soured.

"I did not mean to darken your day."

She shrugged.

For months, Queen Gosea and Curia Benigia had badgered Vinati to dance and woo courtesans. He had ignored their pleas. Only recently had he given in to their demands and danced each night with a seemingly endless parade of women. He never felt the urge to request a second dance.

But something about Pali stirred him. He wanted to lift her spirits as she had raised his. Vinati stood, bowed slightly, and held out his hand. "Come. Let us dance and forget about the Prince and duty. If only for an afternoon."

Pali looked like she would take his hand but scoffed. "There is no music, silly."

Vinati hummed a lively tune. "We shall make our own."

Pali's eyes sparkled again, and she took his hand as she tossed her hair ribbons to the bench.

The Palace hired dance tutors to train Vinati in the art of dance since he was a child. Graceful and lithe, he was a capable dancer. He placed a hand gently at Pali's waist, took her other hand in his. He swept her effortlessly in a graceful arc around the garden while humming.

Pali giggled and joined his singing. She was light on her feet and easily kept pace with the Prince.

"You dance well. For someone who only recently became a courtesan, I mean," Vinati said.

She gazed up at him, her dark brown eyes twinkling. Pali removed his hat and tossed it aside without missing a step. She deftly pulled the cord from his braid, and his long hair tumbled to his shoulders.

"And you dance well for a simple farmer."

Heat prickled his neck. "Um, yes, well—" *She recognizes me. My game is done. Did she speak the truth? Or did she toy with me this whole time?* "When did you know?"

"Only when we began to dance." She glanced up at him furtively. "I've watched you dance from the sidelines. You did not notice me. Simple Pali. Not the fairest or most polished. Country woman Pali. Unlikely to be chosen by the Queen Mother."

"That's not—"

Pali laughed. "You know it's true." She smiled. "But as soon as we began dancing, I knew it was you. You dance like—a prince."

In Pali's smiling eyes, Vinati saw a future he could embrace. One that would make his father, now enmeshed in the roots of the tree of life, proud.

Vinati pulled Pali closer. "Soon, I shall dance like a king. Will you join me for the dance of a lifetime? Will you become my queen, Palomisia?"

Of course, Pali said yes and joined in binding with Vinati the next day. Queen Gosea disapproved of his choice. But with the realm's life in the balance, she could not impede the union.

A year has since passed, and the kingdom of Bardivia now prospers. The vines are again green, and the wells run with Enara's clear waters.

Prince Vinati opened the doors to his solar and welcomed Juka's light spring breezes. "You do not think the cool air will make him ill?"

Queen Pali strode toward him, bouncing a wee swaddled babe as she hummed a sweet melody. "My village bruxia always encouraged babes to take in the fresh air. Said it made their lungs strong." She handed their son, Nérandu II, to his father.

King Vinati took his son gently in his arms, his smile wide. "I never tire of gazing at his perfect face." Vinati joined Pali's song.

Queen Pali held Nérandu's tiny hand in hers. "You have done well, my King. The land prospers once again, as do we." She tilted her head up and received his kiss.

Their balcony doors opened to the Peacock Garden, once again lush with verdant grasses and spring flowers blooming. From their vantage point, Vinati watched Amantu tending to his baby peacocks.

Amantu squawked at Vinati, then chased after one of his brood. Vinati laughed, and Pali joined in his mirth.

"Do you ever miss it? Your carefree life with Amantu?"

Vinati looked wistful, but only for a moment. He gave Nérandu a gentle squeeze and kissed Pali again, deeply this time. "No, my love. For every sunset, there is a sunrise."

Notes

Thundering

I penned the first poem in this collection, *Thundering*, while writing **Season of the Dragon**. I wrote the opening chapter of *Season* several times, but none satisfied me. When I feel stuck, I often use poetry to find my way.

In this instance, Thundering inspired the first line of **Season of the Dragon**:

"Quen's two hearts drummed an uneven rhythm, matching the thunder of the approaching herd."

When I hit on the imagery of the thundering herd matching her two hearts, it was an "Aha!" moment. I knew I could work with it.

The poem also serves as an abstracted blueprint for the entire series. Watch for themes of roots, thunder, awakening gods, and the idea that "We dance in the mud we make."

The Saga of Ilkay

The idea for the short story, *The Saga of Ilkay*, came to me while writing **Season of the Dragon**. Initially, it was just the book that Quen found burned in the ashes of her home. But as I wrote, *The Saga of Ilkay* became embedded in Quen's backstory—a childhood story that she sometimes recalled to bolster her courage.

When I penned the short story, it revealed details about a prominent character that folds back into the lore of the story world. Ilkay's encounter with a certain fire dragon thus influenced the lore of the Rajani, Volenex, and the Dragos Sol'iberi.

To Dance With Lumine

This story in verse was one of the first things I wrote in this series—initially penned in 2015! The poem reveals some of the process used to develop the primary religion followed by people in the Sulmére.

I always enjoyed the idea of personification of gods, such as in Greek mythology. You may recognize that concept in **Season of the Dragon**. In the poem, *To Dance with Lumine*, I played with the idea of gods personified by people. The poem also inspired the origin story for the gods of the Vaya di Soli religion.

The Prince and the Peacock

The last story in this volume is wholly new and not part of my process for writing *Season of the Dragon.* Instead, the story hints at future books in the series. I don't want to reveal spoilers, so I'll leave you with anticipation of the mystery of how this story relates to what's coming in the Dragos Primeri series.

One Last Note

I have one last note about *The Saga of Ilkay* and *The Prince and the Peacock.* These stories are written as legends and lore Quen (and Rhoji) grew up with. Writing these stories helped me learn more about the culture in which Quen and Rhoji were raised.

Children's stories often reflect cultural norms and values. We often teach children societal norms via stories.

Thus, these stories do not reflect what I, the author, think our societal norms should be. Rather, they serve as tools to help me understand the norms of my characters' culture. The question for the characters is whether they will abide by and conform to these ideas. Or will they rebel against the ideals of their society?

I include the stories here for readers who want a deeper understanding of the characters you meet in *Season of the Dragon* and future installments in the Dragos Primeri series.

ACKNOWLEDGMENTS

Thank you to my subscribers, fans, and followers on social, reviewers, and booksellers for supporting this series!

This book would not be possible without the fantastic art from talented artists. Thank you to Braken for creating another beautiful cover that perfectly captures the "vibe" I requested. Thank you also for making the dragon line drawing and tree illustrations throughout the book.

Thank you to Felix for vividly illustrating one of my favorite characters, Oshon'Zahar, and bringing the "impossible" Vahgrin to life! Since Vahgrin is from my imagination and not quite like "reference" images of dragons, he was a challenge. Thank you for interpreting "huge lizard with wings and hair!" I love what you created, and now there *is* a reference image.

Thank you to Angelina for creating area-focused maps and illustrating *To Dance with Lumine*. And thank you to Caitlin for the last story's beautiful illustration of Amantu the peacock.

Thank you, my dear friend Robyn, for being the best writing pal in the world. It's all a bit easier knowing you are in the "trenches" with me. And thank you, as always, to JRF for your unwavering support of my work.

THANK YOU READERS

Thank you for spending valuable time in the world I created! And thank you for reading *Season of the Dragon* and, *The Saga of Ilkay and Collected Stories*. I hope you enjoyed your extended adventure in Menauld.

Search for the Spring Dragon, Dragos Primeri #2, is slated for release in early 2025. The remaining three primary volumes are planned to be released yearly after that. I also plan additional collections of companion stories to enhance the immersive experience of the Dragos Primeri story universe.

To ensure you never miss a new release and be first for cover reveals, etc., become a Subscriber.

SUBSCRIBE:

Authors rely on word-of-mouth to spread news of their books. If you enjoyed *Season of the Dragon* and *Saga of Ilkay (And Collected Stories)*, I appreciate it if you tell your friends, family, colleagues, and book clubs. Thank you to readers who have suggested the series to their local librarians and booksellers. And please leave an honest review on Amazon, BookBub, Barnes & Noble, Goodreads, or wherever you purchase or recommend books. Here are some handy QR codes:

AMAZON:

GOODREADS:

BARNES & NOBLE:

BOOKBUB:

If you enjoy my writing, learn more about my award-winning Sci-Fi series, H.A.L.F.

CAMPFIRE WRITING

Would you like to dive even further into Dragos Primeri? Check out a new story experience happening on the Campfire Writing website. I've been invited to be among the first to publish a new story and worldbuilding experience on Campfire. If you love maps, character backgrounds, story art, backstories, and even more notes from the author, you will love what Campfire Writing has in store. I hope to see you there. Hika!

Milton Keynes UK
Ingram Content Group UK Ltd.
UKHW012153091123
432302UK00003B/18

9 798987 491249